Tumbling riv

W. C. Tuttle

Alpha Editions

This edition published in 2024

ISBN : 9789362517524

Design and Setting By
Alpha Editions
www.alphaedis.com
Email - info@alphaedis.com

As per information held with us this book is in Public Domain.
This book is a reproduction of an important historical work. Alpha Editions uses the best technology to reproduce historical work in the same manner it was first published to preserve its original nature. Any marks or number seen are left intentionally to preserve its true form.

Contents

CHAPTER I: WEDDING NIGHT .... - 1 -
CHAPTER II: "HANGING IS TOO GOOD—" .... - 16 -
CHAPTER III: THE NEW SHERIFF .... - 29 -
CHAPTER IV: RANGE FUNERAL .... - 46 -
CHAPTER V: HASHKNIFE AND SLEEPY .... - 50 -
CHAPTER VI: HASHKNIFE SMELLS A RAT .... - 68 -
CHAPTER VII: CITY *V.* RANGE .... - 80 -
CHAPTER VIII: CLUES.. - 99 -
CHAPTER IX: THE INQUEST .... - 121 -

CHAPTER I:
WEDDING NIGHT

The ranch-house of Uncle Hozie Wheeler's Flying H outfit was ablaze with light. Two lanterns were suspended on the wide veranda which almost encircled the rambling old house; lanterns were hanging from the corral fence, where already many saddle-horses and buggy teams were tied. Lanterns hung within the big stable and there was a lantern suspended to the crosstree of the big estate.

It was a big night at the Flying H. One of the stalls in the stable was piled full of a miscellaneous collection of empty five-gallon cans, cow-bells, shotguns; in fact, every kind of a noise-maker common to the cattle country was ready for the final words of the minister. For this was to be the biggest shivaree ever pulled off on the Tumbling River range.

Inside the living-room was the assembled company, sitting stiffly around the room, more than conscious of the fact that they were all dressed up. Old gray-bearded cattlemen, munching away at their tobacco; old ladies, dressed in all the finery at their limited command; cowboys, uncomfortable in celluloid collars and store clothes; old Uncle Hozie, red of face, grinning at everybody and swearing under his breath at Aunt Emma, who had shamed him into wearing an old Prince Albert coat which had fitted him fifty pounds ago.

"Look like you was the groom, Hozie," chuckled one of the old cattlemen. "Gosh, yo're shore dudded-up!"

"Glad I ain't," said Uncle Hozie quickly. "All them wimmin upstairs, blubberin' over the bride. Haw, haw, haw, haw! She'd ort to have on a swimmin' suit. Haw, haw, haw, haw!"

He winked one eye expressively and jerked his head towards the kitchen. His actions were full of meaning.

Curt Bellew got to his feet, stretched his six-foot frame, smoothed his beard and tramped down heavily on one foot.

"Settin' makes me stiff," he said apologetically. "Got t' move around a little."

He half limped toward the kitchen door.

"Does kinda cramp yuh, Curt," agreed old Buck West.

His wife reached for him, but too late. He didn't look toward her, but followed Curt Bellew.

One by one they complained of inaction and sauntered out.

"I never seen so many men cravin' exercise," declared Mrs. West. "Ordinarily Buck's a great setter."

The women grinned knowingly at each other. They all knew Uncle Hozie had opened the liquor. Aunt Emma came down the stairs, looking quickly around the room.

"Oh, they're all out in the kitchen, Emmy," said Mrs. Bellew. "Said they was gettin' cramped from settin' around."

"Oh, I s'pose Hozie couldn't wait any longer. He swore he'd get drunk. Said he had to get drunk in order to forget that coat he's got on. But he's been pretty temp'rance for the last year or so and a little mite of liquor won't hurt him."

"I s'pose it's all right," said Mrs. West dubiously. "How is Peggy?"

"Standin' it right good," said Aunt Emma. "Never seen a prettier bride in my life. Laura Hatton dressed her, and that girl does show good taste, even if she is from the East."

"I never set no great store by Easterners," said Mrs. Bellew. "But Laura's nice. And she's pretty, too. She's sure put the Injun sign on 'Honey' Bee. That boy ain't worth the powder it would take t' blow him to Halifax. This may sound like an exaggeration, but it's as true as I'm settin' here; Honey Bee cut L.H. on the side of my organ."

"No!" exclaimed the chorus.

"Yessir! With his pocket-knife. Carved 'em right into that polished wood. I said, 'My God, Honey—what'r yuh doin'?'"

"He jist kinda jerked back and looked at his knife, like he didn't know. And then he says:

"'Mrs. Bellew, I begs yore pardon—I thought it was a tree.'"

"He thought it was a tree?" exclaimed Mrs. West.

"Uh-huh. Dreamin', I tell yuh. Thought he was out in the woods."

"Good thing yuh caught him," said Mrs. Selby, a little old lady. "He'd prob'ly put his own initials in it, too."

"Crazier 'n a bedbug!" declared Grandma Owens, whose ninety years allowed her to speak definitely.

"Love, Grandma," said Mrs. Bellew.

"Same thing Annie. I've watched 'em for ninety year, and they ain't no difference—love and lunacy. Has the preacher come yet?"

"Not yet. Listen!"

From the kitchen came the sound of voices raised in song.

"Wa-a-a-ay do-o-o-on yon-n-n-nder in the co-o-orn-field."

"Drunk!" said Grandma flatly.

"Drinking," corrected Aunt Emma. "Most of 'em can stand more than Hozie can, and he ain't drunk until he insists on soloin' 'Silver Threads Among the Gold.' Up to that time he can undress himself and hang up his shirt, but when he starts on 'Silver Threads' he can't even take off his own boots."

"I wish they'd quit before Reverend Lake comes," said Mrs. West. "He might not be in accord with such doings."

"Won't he?" Aunt Emma laughed softly. "Henry Lake may be pious, but he ain't puritanical. If he hears 'em, he'll probably come in through the kitchen. Henry Lake has been givin' us the gospel for twenty-five years, and no man can do that in this country if he goes too strong against liquor."

"Honey and Joe ought to be showin' up," said Mrs. Bellew.

"Oh, they'll be here in time," laughed Aunt Emma. "This is the first time Joe ever got married, and don't you ever think Honey Bee is goin' to be absent when there's a chance to stand up at a weddin' with Laura Hatton."

Jim Wheeler came in from the kitchen and halted just inside the room. He was a big, gnarled sort of man, with mild blue eyes and an unruly mop of gray hair. His new boots creaked painfully and he seemed ill at ease in his new black suit and rumpled tie. Jim and Uncle Hozie were brothers, and Jim was the father of the bride-to-be.

"Preacher ain't here yet?" asked Jim, drawing out a huge silver watch. "It's almost eight o'clock."

"Oh, he'll be here," assured Aunt Emma. "Peggy looks beautiful, Jim."

"Uh-huh." The big man seemed a trifle sad.

"You don't seem to mind losin' yore daughter, Jim," said Mrs. West. "I remember when Sally got married; Buck cried."

"Prob'ly drunk," said Jim unfeelingly.

"Well, I like that, Jim Wheeler!"

A vision in white came down the stairs and halted near the bottom. It was Laura Hatton, the Easterner, who had come to Pinnacle City to attend the wedding of her old school chum. Laura was a tiny little blonde with big blue eyes and a laughing mouth which dismayed every cowboy in the Tumbling River country—except Honey Bee, who had been christened James Edward Bee.

"Wouldn't you ladies like to come up and see the bride?" she asked. "She's just simply a dream. Why, if I looked as pretty in wedding clothes as Peggy does, I'd turn Mormon."

Jim Wheeler watched them go up the stairs and heard their exclamations of astonishment. Out in the kitchen an improvised quartet was singing "Wait till the clouds roll by, Jennie." Jim Wheeler shook his head sadly.

"Don't seem to mind losin' your daughter," he muttered.

Oh, but he did mind it. She would live in her own home. Her mother had been dead ten years. After her death it seemed to Jim Wheeler that nothing could ever fill that void. But Peggy had grown to womanhood, filling the old ranch-house with her joyful presence, and Jim Wheeler had thanked God for a daughter like her. Now she would go away to a home of her own.

"Nobody but me and Wong Lee left," said Wheeler sadly. "And he's only a dirty Chinaman."

Some one was knocking on the door, breaking in on Wheeler's thoughts. He opened the door for the minister of the Tumbling River country. Henry Lake was a tall, lean-faced man, near-sighted, dressed in a rusty suit of black. Weddings, funerals or Sunday sermons, he had worn that suit as long as any of them could remember.

He peered closely at Jim Wheeler, shoving out a bony hand.

"Howdy, Jim," he said pleasantly.

"Hello, Henry. Got here at last, eh?"

The minister nodded slowly.

"My old horse isn't as fast as she used to be, Jim. We're both getting old, it seems. But—" he looked at his watch—"I'm near enough on time. Where's everybody?"

"Wimmin are upstairs with the bride, and the men—" Jim hesitated and glanced toward the kitchen door.

"Carry me-e-e-e ba-a-ack to ol' Virginny," wailed a tenor, while a baritone roared, "While the old mill wheel turns 'round, I'll love you, Ma-a-a-ary; when the bee-e-e-es—"

And then came the reedy falsetto of Hozie Wheeler—

"Da-a-a-arling, I am growing o-o-o-old."

The minister nodded slowly.

"The perfectly natural reaction, Jim. The sentiment contained in corn and rye."

"Like a little shot, Henry?"

"Not now, Jim; later, perhaps. Is the groom here yet?"

"Not yet. Him and Honey ought to be here any minute now."

The women were coming back down the stairs, and the minister went to shake hands with them. Aunt Emma cocked one ear toward the kitchen, and a look of consternation crossed her face. She grasped Jim by the arm and whispered in his ear:

"Shake Hozie loose, Jim! He's silver-threadin' already."

Jim nodded and went to the kitchen.

And while the Flying H resounded with good cheer, while more guests arrived and while Peggy Wheeler waited—Honey Bee buzzed angrily about Pinnacle City. Honey had just arrayed himself in a blue made-to-order suit, patent-leather shoes and a brown derby hat. Everything had come with the suit, and Honey cursed the tailor for having acute astigmatism.

The pants were a full six inches too short and at least that much too big around the waist. Honey managed to squeeze a number eight foot into the number six shoe. And the hat should have been seven and one-quarter, instead of a six and seven-eighths.

Honey Bee was a medium-sized youth of twenty-five, with tow-coloured hair, shading to a roan at the ends, blue eyes, tilted nose and a large mouth. The blue eyes were large and inquiring, and the mouth grinned at everything. Honey was a top-hand cowboy, even if he was somewhat of a dreamer.

But just now there was no smile on Honey's mouth. He had hired a horse and buggy from the livery-stable and had tied the horse in front of the sheriff's office. It just happened that Joe Rich, the sheriff, was going to marry Peggy Wheeler, and had promised Honey to meet him at the office at half-past seven.

Every cowboy in the Tumbling River range envied Joe. Never had there been a lovelier girl than Peggy Wheeler, and none of the boys would admit that Joe was worthy of her.

"It's a love match, pure and simple," Honey had declared. "Peggy's pure and Joe's simple."

But just now Honey was calling Joe stronger things than simpleton. It was nearing eight o'clock, and no Joe in sight. The office was closed. Len Kelsey, Joe's deputy, was out at the Flying H, probably drinking more than was good for him.

Honey didn't like Len. Possibly it was because Honey thought that Joe should have appointed him as deputy. And it is barely possible that Joe would have appointed Honey, except that, in order to swing a certain element, he had made a pre-election promise to appoint Len.

Joe was barely twenty-three years of age. Too young, many of the old-timers said, to be a sheriff of Tumbling River. But Joe won the election. He was a slender young man, slightly above the average in height, with a thin, handsome face, keen gray eyes and a firm mouth. He had been foreman of the Flying H, and Uncle Hozie had mourned the passing of a capable cowhand.

"Plumb ruined," declared the old man. "Never be worth a cuss for anythin' agin'. County offices has ruined more men than liquor and cards."

Honey Bee sat in the buggy, resting his shining feet across the dashboard in order to lessen the pain. The coat was a little tight across the shoulders, and Honey wondered whether the tuck would show where he had gathered in the waistband of the trousers. His cartridge-belt made a decided bulge under his tight vest, but he had no other belt; and no cowboy would ever lower himself to wear suspenders. They were the insignia of a farmer.

"I wish I knowed what kind of a figure that durned tailor had in mind when he built this here suit," said Honey to himself. "I know I measured myself accurately. I might 'a' slipped a little on some of it, bein' as I had to do a little stoopin'; but never as much as this shows. Now where the devil is Joe Rich?"

It was eight o'clock by Honey's watch. He got out of the buggy and almost fell down. His feet had gone to sleep. And when he made a sudden grab for the buggy wheel he heard a slight rip in the shoulder-seam of his coat.

"Gee! I'm comin' apart!" he grunted.

Honey had not seen Joe since about five o'clock, and something seemed to tell him that everything was not right. Joe slept in the office. He and Len Kelsey were together the last time Honey had seen them, and Joe said he was going to get a shave. But the barber shop was closed now.

Honey limped around to Joe's stable and found Joe's horse there. Then he went back to the buggy. It was after eight now, and the wedding was scheduled for eight-thirty. It was over two miles to the Flying H from Pinnacle City and Honey knew that the buggy horse was not a fast stepper.

Honey swore dismally and stood on one foot. He needed a big drink to kill the pain. Across the street was the Pinnacle bar, the most popular saloon in town. There was sure to be several men in there and they would be sure to make some remarks about Honey's clothes.

Farther down the street was the Arapaho bar. Honey did not like the place. "Limpy" Nelson owned the Arapaho, and Honey did not like Limpy. But Honey knew that no one would make remarks about his appearance down there, because Honey's friends frequented the Pinnacle—and friends were the only ones entitled to make remarks.

So Honey stifled his pride and went to the Arapaho, where he leaned against the bar. Old Limpy was the only person there, except a drunk sprawled across a card-table near the rear of the place.

Limpy squinted at Honey and shifted his eyes toward the back of the room as he slid the glasses across the bar.

"Didn't somebody say that the sheriff was gittin' married t'night?" asked Limpy.

Honey poured out his drink and looked at it wearily. Lifting the glass, he looked critically at it.

"Yeah," he said slowly. "I'm waitin' for him."

"That's him back there," Limpy pointed toward the rear.

"Eh?" Honey jerked around, staring. "What's that, Limpy?"

"Joe Rich. Drunk as an owl."

Honey dropped his glass and limped back to the table where Joe Rich sprawled. He slapped Joe on the shoulder, swearing foolishly.

"Joe! Joe, you bleedin' fool! Wake up, can'tcha?"

But Joe merely grunted heavily. He was still wearing the clothes he had worn when Honey saw him last, and he had not shaved.

Dead drunk on his marriage night! Honey sagged weakly against the table, speechless. He could visualize all those people out at the Flying H, waiting for them. He shoved away from the table and looked at Limpy.

"My God, this is awful, Limpy! He was to get married at eight-thirty. It's almost that right now, and look at him!"

"Pretty drunk," nodded Limpy.

"Dead t' the world! Who'd he get drunk with?"

"Alone, I reckon. He was shore polluted when he came here. Got a couple more with Len and went to sleep back there."

Honey groaned painfully. Joe reeked of whisky.

"Oh, you fool!" wailed Honey. "Joe, can'tcha wake up? Let's go for a walk. Joe! A-a-a-aw, you drunken bum!"

Two men came in and walked up to the bar. They were Ed Merrick and Ben Collins. Merrick owned the Circle M outfit, and Ben was one of his cowboys. Merrick had been the one who supported Joe Rich and had asked Joe to appoint Len Kelsey deputy. Len had worked for the Circle for several years.

They came back and looked at Joe.

"And this is his weddin' night!" wailed Honey.

"Gee!" snorted Merrick disgustedly. "He was goin' to marry Peggy Wheeler."

"Loaded to the gills," declared Ben. "He's shore a fine specimen for sheriff."

"Yuh can throw that in a can!" snapped Honey. "Since when did the Circle M start judgin' morals?"

Evidently Ben did not know; so he shut his mouth.

"What are yuh goin' to do?" asked Merrick.

"Put him to bed. My God, I can't take him out to the Flyin' H. Joe! You brainless idiot, wake up!"

"We better help yuh, Honey," said Merrick. "He's plumb floppy."

Honey managed to get the office key from Joe's pocket, and between the three of them they managed to carry Joe back to his office, where they put him on his bed.

"What'll yuh do about it?" asked Merrick when they came out.

"God only knows, Merrick!" wailed Honey. "I can't go out there and say he's drunk. Oh, why didn't the fool get shot, or somethin'? I—I—aw hell, I've got to go out there. I hope to God the horse runs away and breaks my neck. But there ain't much hopes," dismally. "These Pinnacle livery horses never did run away from home. Well, I—thanks for helpin' me put him to bed."

Honey limped out, untied the horse and got into the buggy.

"I'd rather go to a funeral any old time," he told the horse as they left town. "I'd rather go to my own funeral. But it can't be helped; I've got to tell 'em."

It is not difficult to imagine the frame of mind of those at the Flying H when eight-thirty passed and no sign of the groom and best man. The aged minister paced up and down the veranda, trying to make himself believe that everything was all right.

Down by the big gate stood Jim Wheeler, a dim figure beneath the hanging lantern. All hilarity had ceased in the kitchen. Uncle Hozie was seated in the living-room between Aunt Emma and Grandma Owens, grinning widely at nothing whatever.

Upstairs in a bedroom were Peggy Wheeler and Laura Hatton. An old clock on a dresser ticked loudly, its hands pointing at a quarter of nine. Peggy sat on a bed, her hands folded in her lap. She was a decided brunette, taller than Laura, brown-eyed; well entitled to the honour of being the most beautiful girl in the Tumbling River country.

There were tears in her brown eyes, and she bit her lip as Laura turned from the front window, shaking her blonde head.

"Nobody in sight, Peggy. I just can't understand it."

Peggy shook her head. She couldn't trust herself to talk just now. Aunt Emma came slowly up the stairs and looked in at Peggy.

"I'll betcha the buggy broke down," she said. "They'll both come walkin' in pretty soon. Peggy, you dry them tears. Joe's all right. Yuh can't tell what's happened. Bein' the sheriff, he might have been called at the last minute. The law don't wait on marriages. You just wait and see, Peggy."

"Oh, I hope everything is all right," sighed Peggy. "He's twenty minutes late right now, Aunt Emma."

Still they did not come. Some of the cowboys volunteered to ride back to Pinnacle City to see what the trouble might be, when the long-looked for buggy hove in sight. They could see it far down the road in the moonlight. Laura had seen it from the bedroom window and came running back to Peggy.

"Good gracious, stand up, Peggy!" she exclaimed. "Your gown is all wrinkled. They're coming at last. Heavens, your cheeks are all tear-streaked! No, don't wipe them! You little goose, why did you shed all those tears?"

"Well, what would you have done?" laughed Peggy, allowing Laura to smooth her gown.

"I wouldn't cry, that's a sure thing."

She darted back to the window, flinging the curtain aside.

"They've stopped at the gate," she said. "I think they are talking to your father. Now he's coming with them."

Aunt Emma came running up the stairs, calling to Peggy.

"They're here," she called. "Goodness knows, it's time."

"I'm ready, Aunt Emma," called Peggy.

Laura still stood at the window, watching the buggy come up to the veranda. But only Honey Bee got out of the buggy. He was talking to Jim Wheeler and forgot to tie the horse. Then they came into the house. A babel of questions assailed Honey, but Jim Wheeler's heavy voice silenced them. Came several moments of silence. Laura had stepped back beside Peggy, who was listening.

"There ain't goin' to be no weddin'," said Jim Wheeler slowly. "Joe Rich is dead drunk."

A silence followed Jim's announcement. Peggy looked at Laura, and the blood slowly drained from her cheeks. She grasped for the foot of the bed to steady herself. Then came Honey's voice:

"Aw, cuss it, don't look at me thataway!" he wailed. "This wasn't anythin' I could help. I was to meet him at seven-thirty, and he didn't show up; so I waited until after eight. Then I found him in the Arapaho saloon—asleep."

Aunt Emma was coming up the stairs, bringing the news to Peggy. She didn't realise that Peggy had heard all of it. They met at the top of the stairs, and Peggy went past her, clinging to the railing. Aunt Emma touched her on the arm, but Peggy did not look up. At the top of the stairs stood Laura, her eyes wide, the tears running down her cheeks.

Peggy went into the living-room and stopped just inside the doorway. The minister caught sight of her and crossed the room, but she brushed him aside.

"Honey," she said breathlessly, "is that all true?"

Honey Bee shifted his weight to one foot, nodding jerkily.

"My God, I wouldn't lie to yuh, Peggy!" he said. "It shore is hell to have to tell the truth in a case like this. All the way from town I've tried to frame up a lie, but it wasn't no use, Peggy. Mebbe it was my feet. A feller with an eight foot can't think of no lies in a six shoe."

Peggy's eyes swept the assemblage of old friends, and their faces seemed blurred. No one spoke. Her father stood beside her, grim-faced, stunned.

"I'm sorry," said Peggy simply, and went back toward the stairs.

Slowly the crowd gathered up their belongings and went away. Even Uncle Hozie was shocked to sobriety. Finally there was no one left in the big living-room except Honey Bee. He took off his shoes and coat and was going toward the front door when Laura Hatton came down the stairs. She had been crying.

Honey stared at her and she stared at Honey.

"Huh-howdy," said Honey, bobbing his head. "Nice weather."

Then he tried to bow and the effort pulled the waistband of his pants away from his belt. He made a quick grab, and saved the day.

"Oh, why did you have to come and tell her a thing like that?" asked Laura. "Why didn't you lie like a gentleman?"

"Lie like a gentleman?" Honey stared at her, his hands clutching the coat, shoes and waistline.

"Yes—lie!" said Laura fiercely. "You could have told that Joe had to chase horse-thieves, or something like that."

"Uh-huh," grunted Honey. "Well, yeah, I could."

"Well, why didn't you?"

"Them's why!" Honey flung down the offending shoes. "By Gee, you can't be pretty and smart at the same time! Folks say that brains are in yore head, but they're not. They're in yore feet, I tell yuh! Pinch yore feet and yuh can't think. That's why I had to tell the truth."

"I suppose so," said Laura sadly. "Perhaps it is all for the best. You better go home, Mr. Bee; you're half undressed."

"Half?" gasped Honey. "If anythin' makes me let loose—I'm all undressed! Good-night."

Honey climbed into his buggy and drove back to Pinnacle City, sadder and wiser, as far as clothes were concerned. The outfit had cost him forty dollars. He sat down on the brown derby when he got into the seat, but he was too disgusted to move off it.

He turned the horse over to the stableman and went to the Pinnacle Saloon in his sock-feet, carrying his coat. Some of the men who had been at the Flying H were at the saloon, having a drink before going home. Len Kelsey, the deputy, was there. Len was a tall, skinny, swarthy young man, inclined to be boastful of his own abilities.

"You seen Joe?" asked Honey.

Len shook his head.

"Mebbe we better go over and see how he's comin' along," suggested Honey.

They walked over to the office and found Joe still on the bed, snoring heavily. He opened his eyes when Honey shook the bed, and looked around in a bewildered way.

"Whazamatter?" he asked thickly.

"When yuh sober up, you'll find out," growled Honey. "You shore raised hell and put a chunk under it tonight, pardner."

"Huh?"

Joe lifted himself on one elbow and stared at the lamp. He blinked owlishly and looked at Honey. Joe's eyes were bloodshot and he breathed jerkily.

"Whatcha mean?" he asked.

"Do you know what night this is?" asked Honey.

Joe squinted one eye thoughtfully.

"What night? What—" he sank back on the pillow and shut his eyes.

"Pretty sick," observed Len. "Better let him sleep it off."

"Oh, I suppose," said Honey.

He threw some covers over Joe and they went out together, after turning the lamp down low.

But Joe did not go back to sleep. His head ached and his throat was so dry he could hardly swallow. Finally he got out of bed and staggered over to the table, where he turned up the lamp.

For several minutes he stood against the table, rubbing his head and trying to puzzle things out. On a chair near the bed was a white shirt and collar, gleaming white in the light of the lamp. On the floor was a new pair of shoes.

Suddenly the mist lifted from Joe's brain and he remembered. It came to him like an electric shock. He was to be married!

He stumbled to the door and flung it open. It was dark out there, the street deserted. Wonderingly he looked at his watch.

Eleven o'clock!

Slowly he went back to the bed and sat down, holding his head in his hands. What night was it? he wondered. Was it the night of his marriage—or the night before? No, it couldn't be the night before. He remembered everything. And now he remembered that Honey was wearing a white collar. Nothing but a marriage or a funeral would cause Honey to wear a white collar.

He felt nauseated, dry-throated. What had he done? There was a light in the Pinnacle Saloon; so he went over there. The cool night air revived him a little, but his legs did not track very well.

Honey and Len were at the bar, talking with the bartender, when Joe came in.

"Gosh, you shore look like the breakin' up of a hard winter, pardner," observed Honey.

Joe came up to the bar and hooked one elbow over the polished top. He wanted to sit down, but forced himself to stand.

"Honey," he said hoarsely, "what night is this?"

"What night? Joe, you fool, this was yore weddin' night!"

Joe sagged visibly and Honey caught him by the arm.

"You better set down," advised Len.

Joe allowed Honey to lead him to a chair, where he slumped weakly, staring wide-eyed at Honey.

"My weddin' night?" he whispered. "Honey, don't lie to me!"

"Nobody lyin' to yuh, Joe."

Joe slid down in the chair, his face the colour of wood ashes. He lifted his right hand almost to his face, but let it fall to his knee.

"Don't lie, Honey!" It was a weak whisper. There was still hope left.

"I ain't lyin', Joe," said Honey sadly. "Good God, I wish I was! Len was there; he can tell yuh. I waited for yuh, like I said I would, Joe. But you never showed up. It was after eight o'clock when I went huntin' yuh, and split yore hide, I found yuh in the Arapaho, drunk as a boiled owl."

"Drunk as a boiled owl," whispered Joe.

"Y'betcha. I couldn't take yuh, Joe. I'd do anythin' for yuh, and you know it; but I couldn't take yuh out there that-away, so I put yuh to bed."

Joe groaned painfully.

"They—they were out there—everybody, Honey?"

"Everybody, Joe. I tried to think up a lie to tell 'em, but my feet hurt so bad that I couldn't even think. I had to tell 'em the truth. It was nine o'clock. Aw, it was awful."

Joe had sunk down in the chair, breathing like a runner who had just finished a hard race.

"I seen Peggy," said Honey. "My! but she was beautiful! And you hurt her, Joe. I could tell she was hurt bad, but she jist said she was sorry."

"Oh, my God, don't!"

Joe lurched out of the chair, panting, hands clenched. Suddenly he flung his hands up to his eyes.

"Oh, what have I done? I don't understand it. I must have been crazy. Am I crazy now—or dreaming? No, I'm not dreamin'; so I must be crazy. Dead drunk on my weddin'—oh, what's the matter with the world, anyway?"

He stood in the middle of the saloon, his eyes shut, his face twisted with the pain of it all. He stumbled forward and would have fallen had not Honey grasped him.

"You better go and sleep on it, pardner," advised Honey.

"Sleep? With this on my mind?"

"Well, yuh got drunk with it on yore mind."

"Aw, don't rub it in on him," said the bartender. "Better have a drink, Joe. You sure need bracin'."

"He don't need any more drinks," declared Honey. "Good gosh, he plumb reeks of it yet. What he needs is sleep."

"Sleep?" Joe smiled crookedly. "Oh, what can I do? I feel like I was all dead, except my mind."

"Come out to the ranch with me, Joe," urged Honey.

"And face the Bellew family?"

"You've got to face 'em all, sooner or later, Joe."

"I suppose that's true! Honey, what did they say? What did they do?"

"What could they do, Joe? I don't think they said much. I know Peggy didn't. They jist acted like they was stunned. It was worse'n a funeral."

"Hozie was drunk, and it sobered him," offered Len.

"Poor old Hozie," said Joe. "All my friends—once."

"Aw, they'll get over it, Joe," said Honey. "They all like you awful well."

"Did like me, Honey. Oh, I'm all through. I may not have any brains, but in spite of what I've done, I've got some pride left. I can't face 'em. I know what they're saying!

"'Drunken bum! Drunken bum!' Oh, I know it, Honey. No matter whether I'm guilty or not, I'll always be the drunken bum who forgot his own weddin'. Is there anybody or anythin' lower than I am?"

"You could put on a plug-hat and walk under a snake's belly," said Honey unfeelingly. "I'm not upholdin' yuh, cowboy. Far be it from me to interrupt yuh when yuh start sayin' mean things about yourself; but that don't alter the fact that I'm yore friend, and I ask yuh to come out to the bunk-house and sleep yourself into a sane frame of mind. Right now yo're as crazy as a locoed calf."

Joe shook his head.

"Thank yuh, Honey, but I'm goin' to saddle my horse and see if the wind will straighten me out. I'm sick as a fool, and I've got a lot of thinkin' to do."

Joe lurched out of the saloon and stumbled across the street, heading for his stable. Honey shook his head sadly and went back to the bar.

"He's shore sufferin'," said the bartender.

"Yeah, he is," nodded Honey sadly. "He's gittin' all the hell a man ever gits. Yuh don't have to die a sinner to get punished, I happen to know. Some gits it right here."

"Have you suffered?" asked the bartender.

"What in hell do yuh think I'm runnin' around in my socks for? I'll say I've suffered. Let's have one more drink."

CHAPTER II:
"HANGING IS TOO GOOD—"

Pinnacle City was the oldest settlement in the Tumbling River country and had always been the county seat since the boundary lines had been drawn. Originally the place had been only a small settlement and the houses had been built along a wagon-road. And as the place grew larger this road became the main street, with very little added to the original width. In several places the road had twisted to avoid a mud-hole, and the main street was consequently very crooked.

But Pinnacle City had never become a metropolis. It was still the small cow-town; muddy in winter, dusty in summer, with poorly made wooden sidewalks. The railroad had added little to Pinnacle City except a brick-red depot warehouse and some loading corrals.

Eighteen miles southeast was the town of Kelo, and twelve miles northwest was the town of Ransome. Tumbling River ran southwest, cutting straight through the centre of the valley. A short distance west of Pinnacle City were the high pinnacles of the Tumbling range, which gave the town its name. Barbed-wire had never made its appearance in the Tumbling River range, feed was good and there was plenty of water.

Five outfits ranged their stock in the Pinnacle City end of the Tumbling River range, the farthest away from town being Ed Merrick's Circle M, located about eight miles due south. Midway between the town and the Circle M, and just on the east bank of Tumbling River, was Jim Wheeler's HJ ranch.

Southwest, about three miles from town, was Curt Bellew's Lazy B. This was on the west side of the river. A little less than three miles to the northeast of Pinnacle City was Uncle Hozie Wheeler's Flying H; and four miles northwest of town was Buck West's 3W3 outfit.

Jim Wheeler's ranch was just between the wagon road and the railroad, on the way to Kelo. The two bridges were less than half a mile apart. Jim Wheeler's wife had died when Peggy was a little slip of a girl but Jim had kept his ranch and raised his daughter, aided and abetted by Aunt Emma Wheeler, who had wanted to raise her. The HJ was a small ranch. Jim had been content to run a few cattle and horses. Wong Lee, the Chinese cook, had been with the HJ for years, and Jim swore that the county had always assessed Wong as personal property of the HJ.

Uncle Hozie Wheeler's Flying H was a larger outfit, employing three cowboys, Lonnie Myers, Dan Leach and "Nebrasky" Jones, known as the "Heavenly Triplets," possibly because there was nothing heavenly about any of them. Lonnie was a loud-talking boy from the Milk River country; Dan

Leach hailed from eastern Oregon, and Nebrasky's cognomen disclosed the State of his nativity. Uncle Hozie called them his debating society and entered into their State arguments in favour of Arizona.

Curt Bellew's Lazy B supported three cowboys: Eph Harper, "Slim" Coleman and Honey Bee. Mrs. Bellew contended that the ranch could be handled with one man, but that Curt wanted to match Hozie Wheeler in numbers. She pointed out the fact that Buck West could run his 3W3 outfit with only two men, Jimmy Black and Abe Liston, just because Buck wasn't so lazy he couldn't do some of the work himself. Which of course was a gentle hint that Curt might do more, himself.

The Circle M ranged more stock than any of the other ranches and only carried three men besides Ed Merrick. Ben Collins, "Dutch" Siebert and Jack Ralston made up the personnel of the Circle M, since Len Kelsey had left them to take up his duties as deputy sheriff under Joe Rich.

It was the morning following the wedding which had not taken place that Joe Rich rode up to the Flying H. All night long he had ridden across the hills, fighting out with himself to decide what to do, and he was a sorry-looking young man when he drew rein near the veranda of the Flying H ranch-house. He had ridden away without coat, hat or chaps. His trouser-legs were torn from riding past brush, his face scratched, his hair dishevelled.

Uncle Hozie saw him from the window and came down to him. Lonnie Myers and Nebrasky were at the corral, saddling their horses. They merely glanced in his direction, recognising him, but paying no attention. Uncle Hozie looked Joe over critically, but said nothing.

"Well, why don't yuh say somethin'?" demanded Joe wearily. "My God, Hozie, don't just stand there! Swear at me, if yuh feel thataway."

Uncle Hozie shook his head slowly and sighed. He had drunk a little too much the night before and his spirits were not overly bright. A tin can rattled loudly, and they looked toward the stable, where Dan Leach was throwing out the stuff they had stacked in the stall for the shivaree.

Joe's eyes closed tightly for a moment and he turned his head away. He knew what those noise producers had been meant for. A cow-bell clattered among the cans. Lonnie and Nebrasky were watching Joe from the corral.

"I don't feel like cussin' anybody," said Uncle Hozie.

"Not even me?" asked Joe.

"You? Nope. What'sa use, Joe? If yuh cuss folks before they do wrong it might do some good. Afterward, it's no use. Yuh can't wipe out what a man writes in the book of fate, Joe."

"And I shore wrote a page last night, Hozie."

"Yea-a-ah, I'd tell a man yuh did, Joe." Uncle Hozie cocked one eye and looked at Joe.

"There's, by actual count, seventeen blasted fools in this Tumblin' River range—and yo're all of 'em, Joe."

"I admit it, Hozie."

"You do? My God, you didn't think for a minute yuh could deny it, didja? Huh! Why don'tcha git down? My God, I hate to talk to a man on a horse! Especially the mornin' after. Kinda hurts my eyes to look up."

Joe shook his head.

"No, I can't stay, Hozie."

"Nobody asked yuh to, did they?"

"No. Is Peggy here yet?"

"No, she ain't, Joe," softly. "They went home last night—her and Jim and Laura Hatton. Jim thought it was best. Emma tried to get 'em to stay a while, but they kinda wanted to be at home, where there wouldn't be anybody to ask questions."

"To ask questions!" echoed Joe. "That's the worst of it."

"I dunno," sighed Hozie. "It's the first weddin' I ever seen that ravelled right out thataway. Honey Bee showed up with his coat in one hand and his shoes in the other. He shore was the worst-lookin' best man I ever seen."

"Poor old Honey."

"Yeah, yuh ought to feel sorry for somebody, Joe. I don't sabe yuh; by Gee, I don't! I thought I knew yuh, but I reckon I don't. I ain't said what I think about yuh to anybody. Mebbe I ain't had no chance; so many folks has said what they thought about it that I've kinda got their ideas and mine all tangled up. Mebbe after a while I'll git my own ideas straightened up to where I know they're all mine, I'll look 'em over."

"I suppose they'd like to hang me, Hozie."

"Hang yuh? Huh! Reminds me of a Dutchman I knowed. He runs into a gang of punchers that was goin' to lynch a horse thief. Dutchy runs into 'em, and asks what it's all about.

"'Vat iss it all about?' asks Dutchy.

"'Goin' to hang a horse thief,' says a puncher.

"'Oh, dot's too bad,' says Dutchy. 'You shouldn't hang a man for stealing von horse.'

"'It was yore horse, Dutchy.'

"'So-o-o-o? Don't hang him; dot's too good for him. Let me kick him in de pants.'"

Joe smiled bitterly.

"Do you think hangin' is too good for me, Hozie?" he asked.

"I don't say it is, Joe; but when I got a look at Peggy last night I shore wanted to give yuh some of the Dutchman's medicine."

Joe wiped the back of his hand across his cheek and wet his lips with a dry tongue.

"I reckon I'm all through in Tumblin' River, Hozie."

"Well," Uncle Hozie bit off a huge chew of tobacco and masticated rapidly, thoughtfully. "Well, Joe, it ain't for me to say. I got up as far as 'Silver Threads' last night myself, but of course it wasn't my weddin' night. But, accordin' to some remarks I heard expressed last night, the folks of the Tumblin' River ain't takin' up no collection to buy yuh a monument. Yuh see, Joe, Peggy is kinda well liked.'"

"Kinda well liked! My Lor'!" Joe shut his jaw tightly and fumbled at his reins. "I'll be goin', Hozie."

"Yeah? Well." Hozie spat thoughtfully, but did not look up at Joe.

"Be good to yourself," he said slowly.

Joe turned and rode away, never looking back. Hozie sat down on the veranda and Aunt Emma came out. She had been watching from a window.

"What did he have to say?" she asked.

"Joe? Oh, nothin' much."

"What excuse did he offer?"

"None."

"Didn't deny bein' drunk?"

"Didn't mention it."

"Feel sorry about it, Hozie?"

"Didn't say."

"Well, what in the world did you two talk about?"

"Public opinion."

Aunt Emma snorted.

"Public opinion, eh? Did you tell him what you thought of him?"

"Nope; wasn't quite clear in my own mind, Emma."

"I suppose not. If Jim hadn't stopped yuh last night—"

"Oh, I know," Hozie smiled softly. "My voice was kinda good, too. Curt Bellew said he never heard me sing so well."

"Curt was drunk, too."

"Thasso. Prob'ly accounts for him likin' my voice. I'd like to sing to a sober man some day and get an honest opinion."

"No sober man would listen to you, Hozie."

"I s'pose not," Uncle Hozie sighed deeply. "I suppose it's jist sort of a drunken bond between inebriates that makes me feel sorry for Joe Rich, Emma; but I do. He looked so doggone helpless and lonesome this mornin'. No, I didn't tell him I felt sorry. He don't deserve sympathy."

"He don't deserve anythin'," declared Aunt Emma.

"Hangin'—mebbe."

"And you feel sorry for him?"

"I want to, Emma." Uncle Hozie turned and looked at her. "I've worked with that boy a lot. Me and him have rubbed knees on some hard rides, and I kinda looked on Joe like I would on my own son. He was straight and square—until now, Emma. Mebbe," he hesitated for a moment, "mebbe I'm feelin' sorry for the Joe Rich of yesterday."

"Well, that's different, Hozie," said Aunt Emma softly, and went back in the house. She had thought a lot of Joe Rich of yesterday, too.

Joe rode back to Pinnacle City and stabled his tired horse. He had spent all his savings for a little four-room house on the outskirts of Pinnacle and had gone in debt for the furnishings. It was to have been their home.

Len Kelsey was asleep in the office when Joe came in and sat down at his desk. He woke up and looked curiously at Joe.

"Wondered where yuh was, Joe," he said sleepily.

"Yeah?"

Joe drew out a sheet of paper, dipped a pen in the ink bottle and began writing. Kelsey turned over and went to sleep again.

Joe finished writing, folded the paper and walked out of the office. Just south of his office was the old two-story frame-building court-house, and as Joe started to enter the front door he met Jim Wheeler and Angus McLaren, chairman of the board of county commissioners.

McLaren was a big, raw-boned Scot who owned a general store in Kelo. McLaren, Ed Merrick and Ross Layton, of Ransome, composed the board of commissioners.

Joe Rich stopped short as he faced Jim Wheeler. For possibly five seconds the HJ cattleman stared at the sheriff of Tumbling River, and then, without a word, he struck Joe square in the face, knocking him through the doorway, where Joe went to his haunches on the sidewalk, dazed, bleeding from his nose and mouth.

Quickly the big Scotsman stepped in front of Wheeler, grasping him with both hands.

"Stop it, Jim!" he ordered.

Wheeler stepped back, his face crimson with anger, but saying nothing.

Joe did not get up, nor did he even look at Wheeler, who stepped past McLaren and went slowly up the street.

"Are ye much hurt, Joe?" asked McLaren not unkindly. He knew all about what had happened the night before.

Joe did not reply. He got slowly to his feet and leaned against the building, while he drew out the folded sheet of paper. Then he unpinned the silver star from the bosom of his soiled shirt, pinned it to the sheet of paper and handed it to McLaren. Then he turned and went slowly down the street.

McLaren stared after him. Joe Rich staggered slightly, but he was not drunk. McLaren unfolded the paper and read it carefully. It was Joe's resignation, written to the board of county commissioners. McLaren put it in his pocket.

"Life's queer," said the big Scot thoughtfully. "Yesterday he was Joe Rich, sheriff of Tumblin' River, the luckiest young man in the world. And today— nobody! Ye never know yer luck, so ye don't; and who has the right to judge him?"

He turned and went back to his office.

Joe staggered off the main street and went down through an alley. He wanted to get off the street; to be where no one would talk to him. Strangely enough, he felt no pain from the blow. Except for the fact that his face was bleeding, he was not aware he had been hurt.

The thought of Jim Wheeler knocking him down hurt worse than any blow, and he moved along blindly; not going anywhere—just away from everybody. He did not realise where he was until he heard a voice speak his name.

He was standing beside a picket-fence, and there was Honey Bee, holding the reins of his horse. The picket-fence was the one around Joe's house; the one Aunt Emma had called "Honeymoon Home."

"I seen yuh cuttin' across this way," explained Honey. "You shore got an awful lookin' face on yuh, cowboy. Horse kick yuh?"

Joe shook his head. He didn't want to talk with Honey Bee, but he knew there was no chance of getting away from him. Honey was tying his horse to the fence, and now he came over to Joe.

"Mebbe we better go in the house, Joe," he said. "Yuh got to wash off that blood."

Joe nodded and followed Honey to the house. It was not locked. Folks did not lock their houses in the Tumbling River country. Honey filled a basin with water and found a towel. Honey was rather rough but effective.

"Yo're a hell of a lookin' thing," he declared.

"Thasall right," mumbled Joe. "Thanks, Honey."

Joe slumped back in a rocking-chair and closed his eyes, while Honey put away the basin and towel.

"I'm wonderin' what the other feller looks like," said Honey, as he manufactured a cigarette.

"Jim Wheeler," said Joe.

"The devil! Did Jim Wheeler hit yuh, Joe?"

"Yeah."

"Well, I'll be bust! Jim Wheeler! What did he say, Joe?"

"Nothin'. Wasn't anythin' to be said."

"Uh-huh. Makes it kinda hard for yuh, cowboy. Anyway, yuh had to meet him sooner or later. Ain'tcha goin' out to see Peggy?"

"No, I can't do that, Honey."

"I s'pose not. I was past there today—this mornin'. Saw Laura. Didn't sleep none, I reckon. She's a darned pretty girl, but this mornin' her eyes shore looked like two burned holes in a blanket. I pulled off an awful fox pass last night. I took off my coat and shoes, 'cause I shore was in misery, and then Laura comes hoppin' in on me. I has to make my little bow, and my belt missed connections with my pants. Na-a-aw, I saved myself, all right; but it shore needed quick action. Either that tailor is awful cock-eyed, or I'm a queer built jigger."

"You didn't see Peggy?" asked Joe softly.

"Nope. I asked Laura how she was, and Laura asks me how any other girl would be under them conditions. If I was you, I'd go out and have a talk with her. But not the way yuh look now, Joe. Rest up a while. Let Len Kelsey run the office for a few days."

"I resigned this mornin', Honey."

"Yuh resigned? Yuh mean you've quit bein' sheriff? Aw, blazes, why didja do that? You idjit! Throwin' up a job like that. Ho-o-o-o—hum-m-m-m! Joe, yo're a fool."

"In every way, Honey."

"A-a-aw, I didn't mean it thataway, Joe. You know me. I'd go to hell and half-way back for you, and you know it. But you've shore dug yourself an awful hole, and you'll never git out by quittin' thataway. Laura is tryin' to get Peggy to go home with her for a while. She'll prob'ly have one awful time convincin' Jim Wheeler that it's the best thing for Peggy to do—but Laura is shore convincin'."

"You mean that Peggy would go East, Honey?"

"Yeah, sure. She's got friends back there; folks she knew where she went to school with Laura. Mebbe it's the best thing for her to do. Jim ain't got a lot of money, but he can afford it I reckon. What do you figure on doin', Joe?"

"Oh, I don't know, Honey. I can't make up my mind to anythin'. I just run in circles, and every way I turn there's a blank wall; no way out."

"Yeah, I s'pose so. Let's go and buy a drink."

Joe shook his head.

"I don't think I'll ever want another drink of liquor, Honey. I'm goin' to sleep a while, and mebbe I can think my way clear."

Honey came past the court-house and saw Jim Wheeler, Angus McLaren, Ed Merrick and Ross Layton just going into the place. They were going to consider the resignation of Joe Rich, and it did not take them long to decide on an acceptance.

Ross Layton was a saloon owner in Ransome. He was rather small, slightly gray, and affected flowing ties and fancy vests. The rest of his raiment was rather sombre, a fact which had caused Honey Bee to remark—

"Looks like a bleedin' bouquet of flowers wrapped up in crêpe."

There was no argument over the appointment of Len Kelsey as the successor of Joe Rich, and it was up to Len to pick his own deputy. They went from the court-house to the sheriff's office, where they told Len of his good fortune. The skinny-faced deputy grinned widely and accepted his honours. As the three men were leaving Len said to Merrick—

"Send Jack in to see me, Ed."

"All right, Len," nodded Merrick.

Len and Jack Ralston had been bunkies at the Circle M, and it would be the natural thing for Len to appoint Jack as his deputy.

McLaren had some business to attend to at the Pinnacle City bank, so he left Merrick and Wheeler together. Layton had left them at the sheriff's office.

"It's sure funny how things change," observed Merrick.

The owner of the Circle M was slightly under forty years of age, above medium height. He was rather good-looking and dressed well. However, he looked more like a gambler than a county official and a solid citizen. Perhaps this aspect was enhanced by the fact that he shaved regularly, kept his black moustache trimmed and waxed to needle-like points, and wore pants instead of overalls.

"I was thinkin' about Joe Rich," said Merrick.

Jim Wheeler shoved his hands deep in his pockets and did not lift his eyes from serious contemplation of his own boot-toes.

"I wanted to talk to yuh, Merrick," he said slowly. "This sure has been a blow to me. Laura Hatton wants Peggy to go home with her. I dunno—mebbe's it's the best thing to do. I don't mind layin' my cards on the table."

Jim Wheeler looked up at Merrick.

"I owe the Pinnacle City bank seven thousand dollars and I can't ask 'em for any more, Merrick."

"Uh-huh." Merrick did not seem impressed.

"You know what the HJ ranch is, Merrick. Seven thousand is a lot of money against it. I've got to have another thousand, if I send Peggy back with Laura."

"Well, I might let yuh have it, Jim. Bank got a mortgage?"

"Yeah."

"Well, I'll take your note. How soon do yuh need it?"

"Any time in the next couple of days."

"All right, I'll let yuh have it, Jim."

They separated and Merrick went to the Pinnacle Saloon, where he met Honey Bee. Honey had drunk enough to make him loquacious.

"Didja accept Joe's resignation?" asked Honey.

"Nothing else to do," replied Merrick. There was little love lost between these two men.

"Uh-huh." Honey leaned against the bar and cuffed his hat to one side of his head.

"Who'sa sheriff now?"

"Len Kelsey."

"O-o-o-oh, is that so? My, my! Things shore do change quick. If yuh had a lawyer and a doctor in yore Circle M, you'd kinda run the whole danged country, wouldn't yuh?"

"Oh, I don't know," Merrick grinned and invited Honey to have a drink.

"Well, I'll drink with yuh," agreed Honey. "I'm sad at heart." They lifted their glasses to each other.

"Hits Jim Wheeler pretty hard," said Merrick gravely.

"Sure does. Here's how."

"He tells me," said Merrick, placing his glass on the bar, "that his daughter is goin' East with Miss Hatton."

"Yeah, I heard that," said Honey sadly. "I didn't know it was all settled."

"I reckon it is. Anyway, I'm makin' a loan to Jim. He's in kinda heavy at the bank; so I'm lettin' him have the money."

"Uh-huh. Well, that's nice of yuh."

"Where's Joe Rich, Honey?"

"I left him down at his new place, settin' there, lookin' at nothin'. That boy's half crazy."

"Must have been more than half crazy," declared Merrick.

"Yeah. Now I'll buy a drink."

Honey went back to Joe's place before he went to the Lazy B, and found Joe still sitting in the same chair. He told Joe what Merrick had said about Jim's borrowing money from Merrick to send Peggy with Laura.

"How much did he have to borrow?" asked Joe.

Honey didn't know.

"Jim Wheeler must be short of money," said Honey. "Merrick said he was in pretty deep with the Pinnacle bank. They accepted yore resignation and appointed Len Kelsey, Joe."

"Quick work," said Joe shortly.

"Yeah, I'll say it is. You were a fool to quit that job."

Honey left him there and rode out of town. He intended going straight back to the Lazy B, but began thinking about Laura Hatton so strongly that he found himself crossing the Tumbling River bridge before he realised where he was heading.

Jim Wheeler arrived there ahead of Honey, and was sitting on the porch, talking with Peggy and Laura, while Jack Ralston, of the Circle M, sat on a step, hat on the back of his head. Ralston was a tall, curly-headed young man who thought quite a lot of Jack Ralston. He was a clever roper, and one of the best bronc riders in the country.

Honey scowled and wanted to keep right on riding, but he was so close that it might look queer if he didn't stop. Peggy went into the house before Honey arrived. Ralston looked critically at Honey, nodded shortly, and resumed conversation with Laura.

Honey dismounted. Then he uncinched his saddle, shook it a little, and took plenty of time cinching it again. He knew he was of a hair-trigger disposition, and was trying to curb it. Ralston was telling Laura about how he rode Derelict, a locally famous outlaw horse, at a recent rodeo. Honey's ears reddened slightly. Derelict had thrown Honey the day before Ralston had ridden him, and it had taken ten minutes for Honey to recover consciousness.

"It must be wonderful to ride a bucking horse," said Laura. "I saw Lonnie Myers ride one at the Flying H. Oh, it was a lot of fun!"

"That was just an ordinary bucker," said Ralston. "Any puncher can ride a half-broke bucker. Lots of the boys in this country think they're riders, but when it comes to fannin' the real buckers—they don't show much. You wait until we have another rodeo, and I'll show yuh some ridin'."

"Yeah, he's a good rider," said Honey, still fussing with his latigo. "Awful good rider. I shouldn't be surprised if he's half as good as he thinks he is. Ridin' broncs makes folks talk thataway. Of course, us ord'nary punchers don't go lookin' for glory in the bronc corral, so we never do get shook up very bad. But you can tell them good riders every time. They're kinda buck-drunk, as yuh might say. They ain't very tight-brained to begin with, and all that shock and jerk soon gits the inside of their heads kinda rattly.

"Oh, they're all right, as far as that goes. Nobody expects 'em to do anythin' but ride buckers. But they don't know it, and the way them p'fessional bronc riders do talk! Mebbe they ain't so much to blame, at that; but everythin' is 'I' with 'em. Rodeos are all right, I s'pose. Folks get a lot of fun out of it; but them buckin' contests shore do bring in undesirable citizens."

Honey had spoken so earnestly that Laura Hatton did not realise he was talking about Jack Ralston.

But Jack Ralston knew. He got to his feet, glaring at Honey, who paid no attention to him at all. He adjusted the split-ear headstall of his bridle, looked it over critically and came over to the steps. Ralston glanced from Honey to Laura and then shot a glance at Jim Wheeler, who, in spite of the misery in his soul, was trying to stifle a laugh.

"Well, I'll be goin'," said Ralston. "Good day."

Honey twisted his mouth into a wide grin as he watched Ralston ride away.

"He is very entertaining," said Laura.

"Who—Jack?" Honey grinned widely. "Liars mostly always are."

Jim Wheeler laughed and went into the house, for which Honey thanked him mentally. Honey sat down on the steps, cuffed his hat to the back of his head and sighed deeply.

"How's Peggy feelin'?" he asked.

"Better. She's going back home with me; it's all settled."

"Uh-huh," said Honey gloomily. "Lotta luck in that for me."

"For you?"

"Yeah; you goin' away."

"Oh!" Laura's blue eyes opened wide. "Well, you knew I was only here on a visit, Honey."

"Oh! shore; I knowed it. Yuh can't stay, huh?"

"Not very well."

"Uh-huh. I s'pose—" Honey hesitated awkwardly. "I s'pose you've got a lot of fellers back East, eh?"

He pointed north, but the direction made no difference. Laura smiled.

"Fellows? A few—perhaps."

"Uh-huh." Honey scuffed a heel against the step, rattling his spur-chain. "I s'pose you'll be gettin' married, huh?"

"When?"

"Oh, some of these days," gloomily.

Laura shook her pretty head violently. "You bet I won't! After what happened last night I wouldn't marry the best man on earth."

"I'm shore glad to hear yuh say that," said Honey seriously.

"Why?" demanded Laura quickly.

"'Cause if yuh marry the man I hope yuh will, yuh shore won't be gettin' the best man in the world."

Laura blushed and got to her feet. Honey got up, too, and they faced each other.

"You ain't sore, are yuh, Laura?" he asked.

She shook her head slowly.

"No, Honey; I can't get mad at you—but I do think you are awfully funny."

She turned and walked into the house. Honey stared at the doorway for several moments before going back to his horse.

"She thinks I'm awfully funny," he told his horse. "I must be—she didn't even crack a smile."

CHAPTER III:
THE NEW SHERIFF

The following morning Joe moved his few effects from the sheriff's office. Kelsey had just appointed Jack Ralston to act as his deputy, and was showing him where everything was in the office. Kelsey was inclined to be a little superior, and did not shake hands with Joe.

"What do yuh figure on doin', Joe?" asked Ralston.

"Haven't figured anythin' yet, Jack. Probably leave in a few days."

Kelsey did not ask any questions, nor did he look up from the desk when Joe went away. Joe took his belongings down to his little cottage, where he selected the few things he would take with him. He would turn the furniture and carpets back to the Pinnacle Merchandise Company and let somebody handle the sale of the house.

Later on he went up the street, intending to see about having the furniture taken back, when he saw Jim Wheeler and Ed Merrick standing in front of the Pinnacle Saloon. It suddenly struck Joe that this would be a good chance to go out to the HJ and see Peggy. He was ashamed even to face her, but he would feel like a dog if he went away from Tumbling River without seeing her again.

He turned and went to his stable, where he saddled his horse and rode away. There were times during his journey out there when he turned back. But he cursed himself for being a coward and went on. He was not going to ask her to forgive him. That idea had never entered his head.

Peggy was alone on the porch, sitting deep in an old rocking-chair, and did not see Joe until he came up the steps. She started to get up, but sank back, staring at him. Then the tears came and she threw one arm across her face.

"Don't cry," begged Joe. "Curse me, Peggy. I can stand it. I came out here to be cursed—and to say good-bye. I haven't any excuse that you or anybody else would believe; so I'm not askin' anythin'—not excusin' myself. But I didn't want to go away without seein' yuh again."

"Oh, why did you do it, Joe?" she sobbed. "Why? Why?"

"I dunno, Peggy. It's done. There ain't anythin' I can do to make it any different than it is. What's the use of me sayin' I'm sorry? I've been to hell since that night, and it's a rough road. But I just want yuh to tell me good-bye. It ain't much to ask, even after what I've done. Just a good-bye, Peggy."

But she did not speak. Joe's face was the colour of wood ashes as he turned and went down the steps to his horse. For several moments he leaned against his horse, looking back at her, but she had not moved. She was just a huddled heap in the old chair. The sunlight slanted under a corner of the porch, striking across her hair.

He shut his lips tightly, swung into the saddle and rode slowly away. Peggy stirred. Laura had come to the doorway. She had been inside the living-room, listening.

"Where are you going, Joe?" asked Peggy softly. It was hardly more than a whisper. Laura looked curiously at her, wondering.

"You're not going away—to stay, Joe?" said Peggy.

"He's gone, Peggy," said Laura. "Didn't you know?"

Peggy looked up quickly, blinking the tears from her eyes, staring at Laura.

"Gone?" she asked.

"My dear, he went away after he asked you to tell him good-bye," said Laura. "Didn't you know he went away?"

"I didn't know, Laura."

Peggy got to her feet and went to the side porch-railing. Far down the road toward the river bridge was a little cloud of dust which showed the passing of Joe Rich. Peggy turned and looked at Laura, but neither of them spoke. Joe Rich had gone away without even a good-bye from the girl who still loved him; so there was nothing left to say.

Uncle Hozie Wheeler and Lonnie Myers were heading for the HJ ranch. They had crossed the railroad right-of-way at an old wagon-road crossing and struck the HJ road about half a mile west of the Tumbling River bridge. One of the boys had heard that Peggy was going East, and Aunt Emma rushed Hozie right down there to see whether there was any truth in the report. Uncle Hozie didn't care for the solitary ride; so he took Lonnie along. Lonnie was long, lean, and sad of face, thin-haired and inclined to freckle. He was prone to sing sad songs in a quavering tenor and, besides that certain talent, had a developed sense of humour.

"That's wimmin for yuh, Lonnie," declared Uncle Hozie. "All she had to do was to hear that Peggy figures on goin' away, and she chases us down here. Prob'ly wants to put her up a lunch. Ma's funny that-away. If you've got good sense, you'll stay single, Lonnie. Of course, there ain't liable to nobody pick yuh. You ain't e-legible."

"What's that, Hozie?"

"E-legible? Oh, that's a p'lite word, Lonnie. It means that you wouldn't be worth a lot to anybody. It means that nobody wants to hook a sucker when the bass are bitin'."

"Oh, yeah. Joe Rich was e-legible, wasn't he, Hozie?"

"He was—" said Hozie dryly. "He was a big bass when he was hooked, but a sucker when he was landed."

"Uh-huh. Say, that Hatton girl is shore a dinger. I never did see hair and skin like she's got. I'd be scared to touch her."

"So would I—if Honey Bee was lookin', Lonnie."

"Aw, he jist thinks she's his girl."

"Mebbe. Huh!"

Uncle Hozie lifted in his stirrups and looked down the road.

"What's this we're comin' to, Lonnie?"

It was Joe Rich, dismounted, standing in the middle of the road. Standing against the brush on the river side of the road was Jim Wheeler's horse, and Jim Wheeler was in a huddled heap in the middle of the road.

Uncle Hozie and Lonnie dismounted quickly and went over to him. His right leg was twisted in a peculiar position and his head had been badly beaten. Uncle Hozie dropped to his knees and examined him as quickly as possible.

"Joe, for God's sake, what happened to Jim?" he asked.

"I don't know," said Joe dully. "He—his foot was caught in the stirrup, Hozie. The horse dragged him. I just found him a minute ago. Yuh can see his—his leg's broke."

Joe pointed up the dusty road toward town.

"Yuh can see where the horse dragged him."

The trail through the dust was plainly visible, and the condition of Jim's clothes showed what had happened.

"Still alive," panted Hozie. "Lonnie, ride to town as fast as yuh can. Get a hack and the doctor. We can't move him any other way."

Lonnie ran to his horse, mounted on the run and went racing up the road. It was shady along the road; so they made no effort to move Wheeler. Hozie paced up and down beside the road, his hands clenched.

"Where have you been, Joe?" he asked.

Joe, squatting on his heels beside the road looked up at the old man.

"I was over at the HJ, Hozie."

"Uh-huh. I wonder if there's anythin' we can do? By golly, I never felt so danged helpless in my life. I tell yuh, Joe, he's awful badly hurt."

"Awful bad, Hozie. I'm afraid he won't live to get to town."

"And we can't do a thing."

"Only wait, Hozie. Old Doc Curzon is pretty good. He'll save Jim if it's possible."

It seemed hours before any one came. Len Kelsey and Jack Ralston were the first to arrive. Kelsey looked at Jim Wheeler, listened to what Hozie had to say and then walked up the road, trying to find the spot where Jim had fallen out of his saddle. Ralston squatted on his heels, smoking a cigarette, but had nothing to say.

Then came the doctor, followed by Lonnie driving a livery team hitched to a spring-wagon. Several cowboys were also among the interested spectators. The old doctor made a quick examination, after which he placed Jim Wheeler in the bottom of the spring-wagon and started back to town.

"How bad is he hurt, Doc?" asked Hozie anxiously.

"Pretty bad!" snapped the old doctor. "Leg broke once—mebbe twice. Head battered up. Lucky to be alive. Be lucky to live. Don't ask questions until I know something."

"Hadn't we better take him home?" asked Kelsey.

"Take him to my place," said the doctor.

Joe mounted his horse and rode up beside Hozie.

"Somebody ought to tell Peggy," he said.

Hozie nodded.

"You want to go, Joe?"

"You know I couldn't, Hozie."

"Sure. Lonnie, you go and tell her. Jist tell her—"

"A-a-a-aw," snorted Lonnie. "Me? Aw, I'd make a mess of it, Hozie."

"Thasall right, Lonnie; it's a mess already. Go ahead."

Lonnie went, but Lonnie didn't want to; and he didn't mind telling the world that his vocation was punching cows and not being a messenger of bad news.

"Thasall right, Lonnie," assured Hozie. "I won't forget it."

"'F yuh think I will, yo're crazy," said Lonnie.

Joe and Uncle Hozie rode back to Pinnacle City together. A crowd gathered around the doctor's house, waiting for a report on Jim's condition. But before such a report was forthcoming, Lonnie Myers drove in with Peggy and Laura in a buggy from the HJ ranch.

And when the report did come, it shocked every one. Jim Wheeler had died from concussion of the brain. The crowd moved silently away. Jim Wheeler was one of the old-timers, and his death, as Nebrasky Jones said, was "a ter'ble jolt to mankind of Tumblin' River."

Uncle Hozie took Peggy and Laura out to the Flying H, and Lonnie Myers proceeded to drink more whisky than was good for him, in order to forget.

"I was in there when the doctor told 'em," said Lonnie. "Leave-that-bottle-where-it-is! I'm the only person that knows when I've got enough. Jist like a marble statue, that girl was. Didn't say nothin', didn't do nothin'. Say! Why don'tcha git some liquor that's got stren'th?"

"I betcha she feels bad, jist the same," said "Slim" Coleman, of the Lazy B. Slim wasn't very bright.

Lonnie looked pityingly at Slim.

"Oh, I s'pose she does, Slim. If I was in yore place, I'd go away before I tromp yuh to death."

"Aw, you ain't goin' to tromp nobody, Lonnie; yo're drunk."

"I ain't, but I will be," solemnly. "And when I do git drunk, I'll prob'ly forget that yo're jist plain ignorant, Slimmie. Now, you better go spin yore rope where I can't see nor hear yuh."

Nebrasky Jones joined Lonnie, and within an hour Dan Leach rode in from the Flying H. Uncle Hozie and the girls had reached the ranch and Dan said there was too much grief for him; so he came to town.

And thus the Heavenly Triplets got together. Nebrasky and Lonnie were far ahead of Dan, so far as drinks were concerned, and were already given to short crying spells. Lonnie insisted on repeating the story of how they found Joe Rich with Jim Wheeler. According to Lonnie's varying stories, they found Joe and Jim everywhere along the road from the Tumbling River bridge to Pinnacle City.

Time after time he explained how he had broken the bad news to Peggy and Laura. His diplomacy was wonderful to hear, and some of his speeches left him breathless. When as a matter of fact he had said to Peggy:

"Jim's been dragged and they're takin' him to town. Dunno how bad he's hurt, but he shore looks dead to me."

Dan had been with them about an hour when Kelsey came to the Pinnacle bar. Lonnie looked upon him with great disfavour. Joe had been a particular bunkie of the Flying H boys, and they were still loyal. No matter if Joe had resigned voluntarily they felt that Len Kelsey was to blame.

Len walked back among the tables, where he talked to "Handsome" Harry Clark, who owned the Pinnacle. Harry was not handsome by any known standard of beauty, being a hard-faced, sandy-haired individual, with a crooked nose and one sagging eyebrow, caused by stopping a beer bottle in full flight.

"I don' like 'm," declared Lonnie owlishly. "Heza disgrash to—to anythin' what'ver."

"My sen'ments to a i-ota," said Nebrasky. "But what can yuh do, Lonnie? Yo're speakin' of our sher'f, ain'tcha?"

"O-o-o-oh, u-nan-i-mushly!"

"Don't be foolish," advised Dan, who was half sober yet. "He's the sheriff, no matter if he should have been drowned in infancy."

"H'lo, Misser Cold-Feet," grinned Lonnie. "Dan's slowin' up on us, Nebrasky."

"Pos'tively," nodded Nebrasky. "Old boy's showin' age."

"Aw, yo're crazy," flared Dan. "But what can yuh do?"

"Flip 'm," said Lonnie gleefully.

The gentle art of flipping a man consisted of two men getting one on each side of the one to be flipped, grasping him by arms and legs, and turning him completely over. It is a queer sensation, but harmless, if done right. Kelsey was inches taller than either Nebrasky or Lonnie.

The boys goggled wisely at each other and waited. Kelsey finished his conversation with Clark and came back past the bar.

"That shore was awful bad about Jim Wheeler, wasn't it?" said Dan Leach.

The sheriff stopped beside the bar.

"It shore was," he said emphatically. "That horse must 'a' dragged him quite a ways."

"It was like thish," explained Lonnie thickly.

He moved to the left side of Kelsey, while Nebrasky stepped back, taking his position at Kelsey's right.

"Me and Hozie Wheeler," said Lonnie, "was ridin'—let 'er go, Nebrasky!"

And before the unsuspecting sheriff knew what was happening he had been grasped by arms and legs and was starting to imitate a Ferris wheel.

Exerting all their strength, the two drunken cowboys managed to swing Kelsey up to where his feet were almost pointing at the ceiling—but there they stuck. Their leverage was gone. Kelsey's six-shooter fell from his holster, and his watch fell the full length of the chain, striking Kelsey on the chin.

Overbalanced, the two cowboys started staggering backward, stumbled into a card-table and went down with a crash, letting the struggling Kelsey drop squarely on the top of his head.

The crash was terrific. Nebrasky went backward, almost to the wall, working his feet frantically to try to catch up with his body, but went flat on his back. Lonnie caromed off the card-table and landed on his hands and knees, yelling for everybody to get out of his way.

But Kelsey suffered most. He had fallen about three feet on the top of his head, and was still seeing stars. Leach, being of a thoughtful turn of mind, kicked Kelsey's six-shooter down toward the middle of the room, where it came to rest under a card-table.

Several of the saloon employees, including Clark, the owner, came to Kelsey's assistance and sat him in a chair, where he caressed his head and made funny noises.

"You boys better go before he wakes up," advised Clark.

"Is that sho?" asked Lonnie thickly. "Shince when did the Flyin' H outfit learn t' run, I'd crave to know?"

"Tha's my cravin', likewise," said Nebrasky, trying to put his hat on upside down. "Whazze-e got any right to git mad 'bout, in the firs' place? Goo'ness, it was all in fun."

Kelsey was rapidly recovering, and he knew what had happened. His right hand felt his empty holster, and his eyes searched the floor. He had heard the gun fall when he was upside down.

"It's under that card-table up there," said Clark.

Kelsey saw it. He got up slowly and went toward his gun, while the Heavenly Triplets walked straight out through the front doorway. Possibly they did not go straight, but they were out of the saloon when Kelsey recovered his gun.

"I wouldn't do anything, if I was you, Len," said Clark. "They were all drunk and didn't realise."

"Didn't they?" cried Len flatly. "Don't never think they didn't. It was all framed up to dump me on my head. I know that gang."

"Better have a drink and forget it, Len."

"Yeah, that's fine—for you. By Gee, you never got a bump like that—and forgot it."

Kelsey walked straight to the street, but there was no sign of the three men from the Flying H. Kelsey lingered for several moments, then went on toward his office, while into the back door of the Pinnacle Saloon came Nebrasky, Lonnie and Dan, as if nothing had happened.

"Kelsey is lookin' for you three," said Clark.

"Kelsey?" Lonnie blinked seriously. "Kelsey? Oh, the sheriff? Lookin' for us?"

"Whazze want?" asked Nebrasky.

"You had better wait and see, Nebrasky."

"Now that's what I call shound advice, Harry."

"I betcha I know what he wants," said Lonnie. "He wants us to turn him the rest of the way over. Ha, ha, ha, ha, ha!"

This guess seemed so good to them that they sagged against the bar and whooped merrily.

Joe Rich, following the announcement of Jim Wheeler's death, took his horse back to the stable and then went to the store where he had purchased his house furnishings and told the storekeeper to take them back, as there was little chance of their ever being paid for.

When Joe came out he met Angus McLaren, the big grave-faced Scotsman.

"Isn't it too bad about poor Jim Wheeler!" exclaimed Angus. "I just heard of it, Joe."

Joe nodded. His nose and lips were still sore from the weight of Jim Wheeler's fist, and his right hand went involuntarily to his sore spots. McLaren noticed this.

"Ye shouldn't bear any grudge now, Joe," he said softly.

"Grudge?"

"Over what he did to ye, Joe."

Joe shook his head.

"I suppose he had plenty of cause, Mac."

"No matter; he's dead now. They say ye found him."

"Yeah, I did, Mac. I was on my way back from the HJ."

"He wasn't dead then?"

"No, not then. Hozie and Lonnie came along in a few minutes. He was alive then, but I think he died on the way in."

While they were talking Len Kelsey came from the Pinnacle Saloon, rubbing his head, and went down to his office.

"Ye knew we appointed Len in your place, Joe?" asked McLaren.

"I hear yuh did, Mac. And Len appointed Ralston, eh?"

"That's it. What do ye aim to do now?"

"I think I'll leave here, Mac. There's nothin' in Tumblin' River for me any more."

"Ye might get on with the Circle M. Merrick will be short one man, now that Ralston is an officer."

"No, Mac; I don't think I'll stay."

"Mm-m-m-m," McLaren considered Joe gravely.

"Joe, I'd have banked on ye. There's a lot more folks in this country that would have bet a million to one that ye wouldn't do a thing like ye done. Why did ye do it?"

Joe shook his head slowly.

"Mac, there's things that I don't even know; so I can't tell yuh anythin'."

"Well, ye were drunk, weren't ye?"

"Ask Honey Bee, Ed Merrick, Ben Collins or Limpy Nelson. They all saw me, Mac. That should be evidence enough."

"Ay," McLaren sighed. "There seems to be plenty of evidence that you played the fool. I dunno." McLaren took a deep breath and expelled it forcibly. "Well, I wish ye all the luck in the world, Joe Rich. I think you are payin' for yer own sins; but ye are a young man and the world is wide."

They shook hands gravely and Joe went back to his little cottage. It seemed queer that he should be leaving Pinnacle City; almost as queer as the fact that Jim Wheeler was lying dead at the doctor's office. Joe didn't know where he was going, except that it would be out through the south end of the valley; possibly down into Arizona. He would travel light. His war-bag contained a change of clothes, and that was all, except for a few trinkets.

He tied it to his saddle, covering it with a black slicker, and rode up to the county treasurer's office, where he drew a warrant for his remaining salary. Then he cashed it at the Pinnacle City bank, and drew out the few remaining dollars he had on deposit there.

As he came from the bank he met Ed Merrick, who had just tied his horse farther up the street.

"Hello, Joe," greeted Merrick. "What's all this talk about Jim Wheeler gettin' killed?"

"I reckon you heard right, Ed," said Joe.

"Horse drug him to death?"

"Yeah."

"Well, I'll be jiggered!"

Merrick went on down the street, and Joe noticed that he walked fast, as if he was in a big hurry. Joe heard some one call his name, and he turned to see the Heavenly Triplets coming across the street toward him from the Pinnacle Saloon. They were all very unsteady, but also very earnest.

Lonnie sagged back on his heels and considered the roll behind the cantle of Joe's saddle. He sagged ahead and drew the slicker aside enough to disclose the war-bag.

"Where you goin', Joe?" he demanded. "All packed up, eh?"

"I'm pullin' out, Lonnie," said Joe gravely. "I'm shore glad I had a chance to say good-bye to you boys."

"Na-a-awshir," Nebrasky spoke with great deliberation. "Nobody c'n go way like thish, Joseph. Nawshir. Gotta have big party. Misser Rich," gravely, "meet Misser Jones and Misser Leach."

Dan and Nebrasky shook hands seriously with Joe.

"Pleased t' meetcha," said Nebrasky. "I used to know a sher'f that looked like you, par'ner. Oh, ver' mush like you! I slep' in the same bunk with him for two years. You jus' passin' through our fair city, Misser Rich?"

"Just passin' through," said Joe slowly. He saw Merrick and Kelsey leaving the sheriff's office.

"Here comes Misser Kelsey," grinned Lonnie. "'F he gits close enough we'll complete the swing on him, Nebrasky."

"He won't never git close enough," chuckled Dan. "That bird ain't never goin' t' light close to any of us."

Joe held out his hand to Lonnie, who gripped it quickly.

"So-long, Lonnie," said Joe. "Be good to yourself."

"Aw-right, Joe."

Joe shook hands with Dan and Nebrasky, who did it in a dumb sort of a way. Perhaps they did not understand that Joe was leaving Tumbling River. Joe turned to his horse and started to mount. Merrick and Kelsey were close now, and Kelsey said to Joe—

"You ain't leavin' us, are yuh, Joe?"

Joe nodded.

"Yeah, I'm goin', Len."

"Uh-huh. Mebbe yuh better wait a little while, Joe. Somethin' has come up just lately. Better tie yore horse and wait till we get this ironed out."

"What do yuh mean, Len?"

"Has Hozie gone home?" Len spoke to Lonnie.

"Gone home? Of course he's gone home. You seen him leave, didn't yuh?"

Kelsey nodded. Lonnie seemed belligerent.

"When yuh found Jim Wheeler, yuh—uh—didn't look in his pockets, didja, Lonnie?"

"Look in his pockets? What for, I'd crave to ask yuh?"

Kelsey turned to Merrick.

"Mebbe you better go down to the doctor's place, Ed. Mebbe it's still there. I don't reckon anybody looked."

Merrick nodded shortly and hurried away. Joe looked curiously at Kelsey, but the new sheriff was leaning against a porch post, rolling a cigarette.

"Just why had I ought to wait?" asked Joe.

"Just for instance," Kelsey lighted his cigarette.

"That's the new sheriff," said Lonnie. "Cool and collected, always gets his man. Ha, ha, ha, ha, ha!"

Kelsey winced. Nebrasky looked him over thoroughly.

"That's him," declared Nebrasky. "Yuh gotta look close at him to tell. Kelsey is his name, belonged to the Circle M before the county bought him."

"You think yo're pretty smart, don'tcha?" flared Kelsey.

"Don't 'tagonise him," begged Dan.

Joe stepped from his horse and faced Kelsey.

"What's the idea of askin' me to wait, Len?"

"Can't tell yuh yet, Joe."

"Suppose I decided to go ahead?"

"No, I don't think yuh will."

"I'm not under arrest, am I?"

"Not yet."

"Not yet, eh?" Joe laughed recklessly. "Well, I reckon I'll be goin' then."

Joe turned back to his horse.

"Yo're not goin'!" snapped Kelsey.

Joe whirled quickly. Kelsey had half-drawn his gun. It was a foolish move on Kelsey's part; he should have covered Joe, if he wanted to hold him badly enough to resort to a gun-play. Joe did not hesitate. His right hand jerked upward and he fired from his waist.

Kelsey's gun was out of the holster, but his hand flipped open and the gun fell to the sidewalk. He staggered backward, clutching his right forearm, while Joe swung into his saddle and rode swiftly out of town, heading south.

The revolver shot attracted plenty of attention, and it also served to sober the Heavenly Triplets. Kelsey swore bitterly as he clawed away his shirt sleeve. The heavy bullet had ploughed its way through the muscles of his forearm, but did not touch the bone. The shock of it had caused Kelsey's hand to jerk open, releasing his gun.

Folks were crowding in from every direction, trying to find out what it was all about.

"You better pack that arm to the doctor," advised Lonnie.

Kelsey nodded and bit off more profanity. Ed Merrick came through the crowd and quickly got the story of what happened.

"Go and get it dressed, Kelsey," he said, after examining the wound. "No bones broke. Is Jack at the office?"

"Here," said Ralston, shoving his way through.

"Better get on Joe's trail, Jack," said Merrick quickly. "He—you don't need a warrant. Bring him back!"

Ralston ran down the street, while the crowd demanded that Merrick tell them what it was all about. But Merrick merely shut his lips and went to the court-house, followed by Angus McLaren who was as much at sea as any of the crowd.

Once inside their office McLaren asked Merrick what the trouble was all about.

"I'm not accusin' Joe Rich," said Merrick. "But he was the one who found Jim Wheeler. To-day I drew five thousand from the Pinnacle bank and loaned it to Jim Wheeler on his note. He had that money on him when he left town. There is no money in his pockets now, and no one has found any money on him since he came back, or during the time of the first examination. The money is gone, Mac."

"And Joe was the first man to find him," muttered McLaren. "Five thousand dollars! Merrick, that's enough to tempt a man."

"Yo're right, it is! And Joe shot Kelsey in the arm."

"Kelsey was drawin'," reminded McLaren. "The boys say that Kelsey reached for his gun first. Joe wasn't under arrest."

"No, that's true, Mac. But if Joe wasn't guilty, why didn't he stay until it could be cleared up? Ah! there's Ralston!"

Through the window they saw the deputy ride up in front of the court-house, where he talked with several men. Merrick and McLaren went out to him. It seemed as if all the cowboys had disappeared. Ralston spurred over in front of the Pinnacle and went into the saloon, but came out again.

McLaren smothered a grin. The cowboys knew that Ralston would deputise them to ride with him, and they would be obliged to obey his orders; but if he couldn't find them—that was a different matter.

"By God, they all ducked!" snorted Ralston angrily.

"Looks like it," agreed Merrick. "Well, I'll go with yuh, Jack. If we can't do any better, we might find some of the boys at my ranch. I guess they won't sneak out on yuh!"

Merrick crossed the street to the Pinnacle hitch-rack and mounted his horse. Ralston went back to the office and got an extra Winchester for Merrick, and they rode away at a swift gallop.

They had barely disappeared when the Heavenly Triplets showed up. They had rolled under the sidewalk near where Joe had shot Kelsey. From the depths of an empty wagon-box farther up the street came Abe Liston, of the 3W3. Slim Coleman, of the Lazy B, sauntered out of the narrow alley between the Pinnacle Saloon and a feed-store.

The Heavenly Triplets were fairly sober now—too sober to think of anything funny to do; so they headed for the Pinnacle Saloon.

"Hey, you snake-hunters!" yelled Slim Coleman. "Didn't yuh ride away with the posse?"

"We shore did!" replied Lonnie. "Couldn't find a thing. C'mon and have a drink, you man hunter."

"Sheriffin' does make a feller kinda dry," admitted Slim. "I'll go yuh once, if I lose all m'hair. Ha, ha, ha, ha, ha! I'll betcha Ralston is mad enough to gnaw a nail."

"Well, he can go plumb to the devil, as far as we're concerned," declared Nebrasky. "Any old time we go huntin' criminals, it'll be when there ain't nothin' else to do. Anyway, I don't look upon the shootin' of Kelsey as a crime."

They lined up at the bar and offered to sing a song for the drinks. But the bartender was a bit sceptical about the intrinsic value of anything they might sing.

"It's all right with me, yuh understand," explained the bartender. "But when Handsome starts checkin' up the till at night—you know what I mean."

"Oh, shore," nodded Lonnie. "Some folks never appreciate talent. Howja like to have a free song?"

"Oh, I can absorb anythin' that don't hurt the rest of yuh. All I ask is that yuh don't require my opinion. I'm honest."

Angus McLaren came in and Lonnie invited him to share their hospitality. McLaren rarely drank anything, but no one had ever known him to refuse an invitation.

"We just got back from ridin' with the deputy," explained Nebrasky. "Ridin' allus makes me dry."

McLaren laughed and poured out a drink.

"Well, here's hopin' they never even catch sight of Joe's dust," said Leach.

"I dunno," said McLaren. "Ye see, boys, it's a serious charge they've put against Joe Rich."

"Serious!" snorted Lonnie. "To shoot Kelsey? Why, Kelsey was reachin' for—"

"I know that, Lonnie. But that's not the charge. To-day Ed Merrick loaned Jim Wheeler five thousand in cash and took Jim's note for it. Jim rode away with the money. There's not a cent on poor Jim—and Joe was the one who found him."

"A-a-a-a-aw, Gee!" Lonnie dropped his glass on the floor.

"Yuh mean to say that Joe got away with it?" asked Nebrasky.

"I'm not sayin' anythin', Nebr-r-rasky. It was told to me. I went to the bank, and they tell me Merrick drew the money."

"Well, for God's sake!" snorted Lonnie. "That's awful!"

"Aye, it is. Well, here's luck, boys!"

McLaren drained his glass alone. The Heavenly Triplets and Slim had no taste for liquor now. They went outside and sat down on the edge of the sidewalk, humped over like four crows on a fence-rail.

For possibly five minutes they said nothing. Then Lonnie broke the silence with—

"Joe's turnin' out to be a humdinger."

Nebrasky spat dryly and expounded—

"Yuh never can tell which way a dill-pickle will squirt."

"Five 'r no five—I hope he gits away," said Leach.

"I thought there was somethin' funny about him bein' in such a hurry to git away," said Slim.

"And you know yo're a liar, Slim," said Lonnie.

"Yeah, I know it," agreed Slim.

"Might as well go home, I s'pose," observed Nebrasky.

"Yeah, and right here and now I want to proclaim," said Lonnie, "there ain't goin' to be no drawin' straws and all that kinda stuff; *sabe*? I don't care a cuss which one of you two pelicans decide to break the news at the Flyin' H, but

I want yuh to know it ain't goin' to be little Lonnie. By God! I've broke all the news I'm goin' to today!"

"I guess we better not say anythin' to 'em a-tall," decided Nebrasky. "It ain't no settled fact."

"Shore—jist let it kinda drift," agreed Leach.

"There goes Kelsey, wearin' his arm in a sling," said Slim. "He's lucky it ain't his head."

"Come dang near bein'," laughed Lonnie, and he headed for the hitch-rack.

Kelsey swore inwardly at the three punchers and wondered why Ralston didn't deputise some of them to go with him. He met Handsome Clark at the door of a Chinese restaurant, and Clark told him that the cowboys had all disappeared when Jack Ralston showed up, and that Merrick had been the only one to ride with him.

Clark did not know about the missing money until Kelsey told him about it.

"No wonder he plugged you," said Clark. "He probably had all that money on him."

"Probably. It was all in currency—big bills, mostly."

"How's the arm?"

"Don't hurt much. Won't be usin' it for a while. I never looked for Joe to shoot. He's awful fast with a gun."

Clark nodded.

"You drew first, didn't you, Len?"

"Mebbe I did. He said he was goin'. Yuh see, I didn't want to arrest him. There wasn't any sure thing that the money wasn't in Wheeler's pockets. I just asked Joe to wait, and when he insisted on goin' I didn't know just what to do. If I'd had any sense, I'd have poked a gun in his ribs and made him wait. Live and learn, I reckon."

"I suppose they'll get him."

"Mebbe. Joe knows this country and he must 'a' been set for a getaway. Yuh can't tell which way he'll go. Headed out south, but he's just as liable to be ridin' north now. He's no fool. And two men might not be able to find him. We can't expect much help from the punchers."

"No, it seems that you can't, Len. Being a sheriff in Tumbling River has its drawbacks."

Len left McLaren and went to the depot, where he sent wires to Kelo and Ransome, notifying the marshals of each place to watch for Joe Rich. And then he went back to his office to nurse his aching arm and swear at himself for half-drawing a six-shooter on a man like Joe Rich.

CHAPTER IV:
RANGE FUNERAL

Bad news travels swiftly in the range country and the following morning there was quite a gathering of the clan at the Flying H. People came to extend their sympathy to Peggy Wheeler and to the rest of the Wheeler family. Even the Reverend Henry Lake and his slow-moving old buggy horse showed up at the ranch, the minister dressed in his ancient best.

Aunt Emma Wheeler, Aunt Annie Bellew, Grandma Owens and Mrs. Buck West gathered together and talked in whispers of the white-faced girl upstairs who did not want to talk with anybody, while the men stood around at the rear of the house in the shade of the big cottonwood and drank up the rest of Uncle Hozie's wedding liquor.

Honey Bee was there, longing for a chance to talk with Laura Hatton. A little later on Len Kelsey, his arm in a sling, rode out. The Heavenly Triplets were sober, but that did not prevent them from making caustic remarks about the sheriff when they saw him coming.

"You let him alone," ordered Uncle Hozie. "Ain't there trouble enough, without you startin' a debate with the law? Lonnie, you haul in yore horns; *sabe*?"

"Aw, he gives me a itch," growled Lonnie.

"Go scratch yourself," advised Uncle Hozie.

Kelsey brought no news of Joe Rich. He said that Ralston and Merrick had ridden through to Kelo, but found no trace of the fugitive. Ralston had come back to Pinnacle City at midnight.

"Yuh didn't expect to catch him, didja?" asked Nebrasky.

"Sure we'll get him," confidently. "May take a little while."

"Aw, hell!" snorted Lonnie. "You and Jack Ralston couldn't foller a load of hay through a fresh snow."

"Lonnie, I told yuh—" began Uncle Hozie.

"Yeah, I heard yuh," interrupted Lonnie. "I'm not ridin' him."

Len smiled thinly.

"Thasall right, Hozie. You folks have kinda got the wrong idea of all this. I'm not an enemy of Joe Rich. I worked with him, didn't I? In my business yuh don't have to hate a man to arrest him. There ain't nothin' personal about me huntin' for Joe. If he's innocent, he ought to stay and prove it. Yuh can't jist sneeze a couple of times and forget that five thousand dollars are missin', can yuh?"

"No, yuh shore can't, Len," agreed Uncle Hozie.

Len didn't stay long. His speech impressed all, except the three Flying H cowpunchers. They had no real reason for disliking Len Kelsey, except that he represented the law, and that he had succeeded Joe Rich. And they were loyal to Joe, even if he was guilty as charged. Theirs was not a fickle friendship; not something that merely endured in fair weather.

Uncle Hozie talked long and earnestly with the minister over the funeral arrangements, and together they went up the stairs to talk with Peggy. Laura left them and came down to the veranda, where Honey Bee beamed with delight.

"I was scared I wasn't goin' to see yuh," he said softly. "How's Peggy standin' it?"

Laura sighed and shook her pretty head. "Peggy would be all right, if all those women wouldn't sit around and talk about corpses they have seen. They all talk about successful funerals! As though any funeral could be a success! And they all gabble about Joe Rich. Honey, I actually think that some of them believe Joe Rich killed Uncle Jim."

"Eh?" Honey jerked back, staring at her. "Ex-cuse my language, but that's a hell of an idea! Who started that?"

"Oh, I don't know. They talked about Uncle Jim being a good rider and a sober man and that the saddle did not turn. And he had all that money with him."

"Well, I'll be darned!" snorted Honey. "Did Peggy know Jim Wheeler was borrowin' that money from Merrick?"

"Yes. She didn't know how much. Now she says she can't go. They talk about Uncle Jim having a big mortgage at the bank, and with the five thousand from Merrick—"

"Lotta money," mused Honey Bee. "Huh-how soon do yuh aim to leave, Laura?"

"I don't know. Not until after things are straightened up for Peggy. I sent Dad a wire telling him that our plans had been changed."

"Then yuh won't be goin' for a while, eh?" Honey sighed with relief. "That's shore fine. Yuh won't go back to the HJ, will yuh?"

"I think so. Wong Lee is still there and Uncle Hozie said one of his boys could go down there and help run the place."

"Yea-a-a-ah? Uh-huh. Which one, I wonder?"

"I don't know. Uncle Hozie spoke about Lonnie Myers."

"Oh, yeah—Lonnie. Ain't settled yet, eh?"

"No; he just spoke about it a while ago."

Uncle Hozie and the minister came out, talking softly; so Laura hurried back upstairs to Peggy. Honey rubbed his chin thoughtfully and waited for Uncle Hozie and the minister to end their conversation.

And then Honey lost no time in backing Uncle Hozie against the wall.

"Laura tells me that Peggy is goin' back to the HJ, after the funeral, Hozie."

Uncle Hozie nodded slowly.

"She says she is, Honey."

"Yo're a pretty good friend of mine, aint'cha, Hozie?"

"Well—" Hozie pursed his lips and blinked at Honey—"I never throwed any rocks at yuh when yuh wasn't lookin'."

Honey leaned forward and whispered rapidly in Hozie's ear.

"Huh? O-o-oh!" Hozie understood.

A few minutes later Hozie met Curt Bellew near the kitchen door.

"I jist wanted to ask yuh somethin', Curt," said Uncle Hozie. "I—uh—I been talkin' to Peggy. Yuh see, Curt, she's goin' to stay at the HJ, at least a while. Won't be nobody there but her and Laura and Wong Lee."

"Uh-huh."

"Well, I been talkin' to her, yuh understand, Curt. She's goin' to need one man to help run things. I—uh—she said she'd like to have Honey Bee to run the place."

"Oh, yea-a-a-ah!"

Curt lifted his eyebrows thoughtfully and hooked his thumbs over his cartridge-belt. He nodded slowly.

"Well, mebbe I can git along without that boy for a while, Hozie. He prob'ly won't want to do it. Honey's funny thataway. But you tell him I said he had to do it. If he kicks about makin' the change—you tell him to come to me."

"Yeah, I'll do that, Curt," solemnly.

They looked at each other seriously for several moments.

"And that ain't the funniest part of it," said Uncle Hozie. "Laura told Honey that I was goin' to loan 'em Lonnie Myers to run the HJ—and there ain't never been any mention of me loanin' anybody."

"She made it all up, Hozie?"

"'Course she did. Her father's a broker in Philadelphia, and I s'pose Laura inherited her ability to tell p'lite lies from him. But it's all right, ain't it, Curt?"

"Fine! Ma will be glad. She has to watch Honey like a hawk to keep him from cuttin' L.H. on all the furniture."

They chuckled together for several moments. Then—

"Hozie, what's this talk about mebbe Jim's death wasn't an accident?"

"Wimmin," said Hozie quickly. "Old wimmin talkin'."

"Uh-huh. Yeah, I s'pose it is. I don't like it, Hozie. But a while ago I got to thinkin' about Jim. Where's that note? Ed Merrick must 'a' signed a copy for Jim. Merrick's got his copy signed by Jim."

"Whoever got the money must 'a' took the note, Curt."

"I s'pose. The money was all in big bills. By golly, I hope they find Joe Rich."

Uncle Hozie sighed deeply. He loved Joe Rich like a son, and it was difficult for him to believe Joe guilty.

"It hurts Peggy," he said slowly. "It hurts her as much as the death of her father. Yuh see, she loved Joe a lot."

"I reckon we all did, Hozie—up to the day he was to be married."

"Joe Rich of yesterday," muttered Uncle Hozie.

"Whatcha say, Hozie?"

"Jist thinkin' out loud, Curt. I'll find Honey, and break the bad news to him."

"Yeah; he'll prob'ly be sore as hell."

CHAPTER V:
HASHKNIFE AND SLEEPY

It was several days after the funeral of Jim Wheeler, and things in the Tumbling River range seemed back on an even keel again. Joe Rich was still at large. The sheriff had broadcast Joe's description, and the county had offered a thousand dollars reward.

Kelsey and Ralston still searched the Tumbling River hills, hoping that Joe had not left the valley. Even the Heavenly Triplets were too busy to annoy the sheriff, but were looking forward to pay day.

Honey Bee was firmly established at the HJ much to the amusement of every one. Uncle Hozie had never told him that Laura had fibbed about Lonnie Myers' going to run the ranch; so Honey believed Hozie had done him a great favour.

Peggy took little interest in anything. The shock had taken the spirit all out of her, and she realised that it would only be a question of time until the Pinnacle bank and Ed Merrick would own the HJ. Twelve thousand is a lot of money.

Aunt Emma did not like the arrangement at the HJ.

"Them two girls livin' alone with one man."

"Nothin' of the kind," denied Uncle Hozie. "Honey's in love, and a man in love ain't more'n half a man. Anyway, there's Wong Lee."

"A heathen Chinee!"

"He's a Chinaman, but I'll betcha he's as much of a Christian as any of us."

"Anyway," declared Aunt Emma, "I'm goin' to spend all the time I can with the girls."

Aunt Emma was one of those who believed that Jim Wheeler had not died from an accident. She talked with the old doctor about the bruises on Wheeler's skull, and he told her that they were caused by Jim Wheeler's head striking the rocks.

"But how did he fall off?" queried the old lady. "Jim was a good rider, Doc. The saddle never turned with him."

The doctor shook his head.

"I'm sure I don't know, Mrs. Wheeler. I am not a detective. His leg was broken from being hung in the stirrup, I suppose."

"He wasn't hung to the stirrup when Joe found him."

"Wasn't he? Perhaps Joe Rich knows more about it than we do, Mrs. Wheeler."

"Sure—but where's Joe?"

"If I knew I'd be a thousand dollars better off than I am."

But few, if any, of the men thought that it had been anything but an accident. A sudden dizziness, perhaps caused by indigestion, might have made him fall. And the horse, even if it was well broken, might have got frightened and dragged him. But there was no question about his being robbed.

It was the evening of the fifth day since Joe Rich had left Pinnacle City when a long train of dusty cattle-cars drew into the town of Kelo. Dusty, wild-eyed animals peered out through the barred sides of the cars, bawling their displeasure.

The wind was blowing a gale, and to the north an electric storm was coming down the valley. But there was no rain; only wind and a depressed atmosphere which presaged the coming storm. The engine clanked in past the depot and stopped with a jerk that shortened every draw-bar in the long line of cars.

In the caboose of the cattle-train sat a cowboy, humped over on a bench, holding his face in his hands. His broad shoulders twisted painfully and he gave vent to a withering curse when the caboose almost jerked him off the bench.

On the opposite side of the car sat a tall, lean-faced cowboy, his sad gray eyes contemplating the sufferer, who lifted his head, disclosing a swollen jaw. Two other cowboys were seated on the floor of the car, resting their backs against the side-seats, while they industriously shot craps for dimes.

"Hurt yuh pretty bad, Sleepy?" asked the tall cowboy.

The sufferer lifted his head, nodded slowly and inserted a big forefinger inside his mouth.

"Wursh a glew har glog daged dantist libed."

He removed the finger, spat painfully and took his face in both hands again. "Sleepy" Stevens was suffering the pangs of an aching molar. "Hashknife" Hartley, the tall, lean cowboy, nodded understandingly.

"It's worse than I thought, Sleepy," he said, his voice full of sympathy. "You've got what they call a Eskimo abscess."

"Huh? How do yuh know?"

"I can tell by yore talk—pure Eskimo."

"A-a-a-aw! If you had this tooth—"

"We're goin' to water these animals at Pinnacle City," offered one of the crap-shooters. "You'll have time to have that tooth pulled."

"Hadn't ought to be far now," observed Hashknife.

He bent his long nose against the dirty window glass and peered out. The wind whistled past, and the sand sifted through the window. A lightning flash illumined things and a rumble of thunder came to their ears.

A few minutes later a brakeman, carrying a lighted lantern, swung aboard.

"Wires down," he said shortly.

"What'll that do to us?" queried Hashknife.

"Not much. We're late and we ought to lay out here and let Number 4 pass us, goin' north; but we can't get any orders, and the sidin's blocked with a freight that broke an axle. We'll go on to Pinnacle City, and the passenger will have to foller us on a slow order."

"Quite a storm, eh?" remarked a crap-shooter.

"Some storm ahead of us," declared the brakeman, going out again.

Finally the engine sent out its shrill blasts, calling in the flagman, and in a few moments the draw-bars jerked shudderingly. The cattle-train was on its way again, picking up the conductor at the station.

Sleepy groaned and hunched down in his chair. The tooth had been thumping for eight hours. And there was a question in Sleepy's mind about finding a dentist in Pinnacle City. Few of the old cow-towns boasted a dentist, and the local doctor was usually more or less of a failure with forceps.

The long cattle-train moved slowly. There was considerable of a grade between Kelo and Pinnacle City, and the terrific head wind held them back. The conductor and brakeman got into the crap game, trying to kill time over the dreary eighteen-mile stretch.

The train rumbled and clanked along, unable to make much headway.

"Likely blow all the hair off them cow critters," observed one of the cowboys.

The caboose was foggy with dust, and the oil lamps hardly made light enough for them to see the spots on the worn dice.

Suddenly the draw-bars clanked together and the caboose began stopping by jerks. Sleepy swore painfully, when it jerked him upright. The engine whistled shrilly, and the train ground to a stop. The conductor peered out, swore softly and picked up his lantern.

"Must be just about to the Tumbling River bridge," he said.

"How far is it from town?" asked Sleepy.

"Couple of miles," said the brakeman.

He too had picked up his lantern, and they went outside. A moment later the brakeman sprang back on to the steps.

"Bridge on fire," he said. "Lightnin' must have struck it."

He lifted the top off a seat and took out several fuses which he tucked under his arm, picked up a red lantern and hurried out to flag down the track. Hashknife put on his sombrero and climbed off the caboose. It was a long way to the front end of the train, and the wind threatened to blow him off the side of the fill at any time.

The Tumbling River bridge was about a hundred and fifty feet across, built high above the stream. It was mostly of timber construction and one span of it was burning merrily.

Hashknife found the conductor and engineer looking over; both decided that it would be folly to try to run it. It had evidently been burning for quite a while.

"That shore hangs us high and dry, don't it?" asked Hashknife.

The conductor nodded grimly.

"We're here for a while," he said. "Can't take a chance on that thing, and we've got a passenger coming in behind us. They'll be running slow, and won't be hard to flag. The best thing for you boys to do is to go to bed. That span is sure to burn out in this wind."

The wind was so strong that they had to yell in order to converse.

"Might as well be comfortable!" yelled the engineer.

The conductor nodded and followed Hashknife back to the caboose, where he broke the news to the rest of the boys.

"Ain't that pathetic?" wailed Sleepy. "Two miles from a dentist, and the road on fire!"

"Better go to bed, Sleepy," said Hashknife. "Mebbe yuh can sleep it off."

But Sleepy told them in no uncertain terms that sleep was out of the question. One of the cowboys produced a pint of liquor, and this served to put Sleepy in better spirits. No one denied him any of it. Hashknife was curious about the passenger train which was following them, and went on to the rear platform.

Possibly they had been stopped for thirty minutes when Hashknife saw the beams of the passenger engine. The road was fairly crooked for several miles, and he could see the beams of the headlight, as it swung around the curve throwing streamers of light off across the hills. It was not travelling fast. It came closer and closer, and Hashknife wondered why it did not seem to pay any attention to the rear flagman. Of course he was out of sight around a curve, but the speed of the passenger had not diminished.

It swung to the straight track, the beams of the headlight illuminating the rear of the stalled train. It was then that the whistle shrieked and the train quickly ground to a stop about a hundred yards short of the caboose.

A man dropped from the engine and came up to the caboose. It was a uniformed brakeman.

"What's that ahead—a fire?" he asked, swinging up on the steps.

"Bridge on fire," said Hashknife. "Looks like we're here for a while."

"Pshaw! Some wind, eh? Say, I wonder why nobody was flaggin' the rear of this train?"

"They did," declared Hashknife. "I saw the brakeman start back with his fuses and lantern."

"You did? That's funny, we never seen him."

The conductor came out and corroborated Hashknife. In a few minutes the conductor of the passenger came along. He was a fussy little fat man, very important. He wheezed his profanity.

"Can't get across, eh? Gee! Wires down behind us. Nothing to do but wait. How did it happen you didn't send out a flag? We might have rammed you."

"Flag went out!" snapped the freight conductor.

"We didn't see it," said the brakeman. "I was in the cab."

"Anyway, he went back," declared the freight conductor. "It's no fault of mine if you fellows can't see."

"Any chance of putting the fire out?" asked the passenger conductor.

"Not a chance. One whole span on fire and this wind is like a blow torch. Looks like a complete tie-up for this division. There's a section crew at Pinnacle City, but this will be a job for bridge builders."

Hashknife went back in the caboose where Sleepy was lying on a seat, still caressing a sore jaw.

"Stuck completely," said Hashknife. "No dentist for you tonight, cowboy."

The brakeman came in to light a cigarette and Hashknife questioned him about Pinnacle City.

"South of here is the wagon bridge," said the brakeman. "I ain't familiar with this country, so I can't tell yuh how far it is, but it can't be a mile—not over that, anyway."

He went out, and Hashknife turned to Sleepy.

"How about yuh, cowboy? It ain't over three miles to town. Suppose we walk over and find a dentist?"

"I'd do anythin' to stop this ache, Hashknife!"

"All right."

Hashknife went down the car, where he picked up their war-bags and brought them back.

"You ain't pullin' out for keeps, are yuh?" asked one of the crap-shooting cowboys.

"Nope," grinned Hashknife. "We'll meet yuh in Pinnacle City. Only a fool walks away and leaves his war-bag. Yuh never know what's ahead of yuh."

He dug down in his bag and drew out a well-worn cartridge-belt to which was attached a scarred holster containing a heavy Colt revolver. He looped the belt around his lean hips, yanked the buckle together and proceeded to fill the cylinder with .45 cartridges.

Sleepy released his jaw long enough to buckle on his own armament, and swung the bag over his shoulder and they went out into the night. The train crew had left the caboose steps as the two cowboys swung down off the fill and stumbled their way to the barb-wire fence of the right-of-way.

"Blacker'n the inside of a cat," declared Sleepy, after they were away from the lights of the train. "Look out yuh don't fall off the river bank."

"It shore is kinda vague," said Hashknife. "Jist take it easy."

"Ain't nobody breakin' into a gallop," retorted Sleepy.

They were travelling through a thicket of jack-pines, which whipped them across the face and tangled their feet. The wind was still blowing furiously, and there was a spit of rain in the air.

Hashknife was surging ahead, one hand flung up to protect his face from the whipping branches, when he almost ran into some object. It flashed into his mind that it was a range animal, perhaps a horse. Sleepy bumped into Hashknife and stopped with a grunt.

Then came the flash of a gun, a streak of flame that licked out into the wind not over fifteen feet from them. The wind seemed fairly to blow the report away from them. It was little more than a sharp pop.

Hashknife stumbled over a little jackpine and went to his knees while Sleepy unceremoniously sat down. And then the animal was gone. Evidently it had borne a rider. The wind prevented them from hearing which way it went.

Hashknife crawled back and found one of Sleepy's boots.

"Didn't hit yuh, did it?" yelled Hashknife.

"No! What do yuh make of it?"

"Queer thing to do, Sleepy."

They got back to their feet.

"How's the tooth?" asked Hashknife.

"Tooth? Oh, yeah. Say, I forgot it. Let's go."

They went ahead again, stumbling along while the rain increased, and they began to be very uncomfortable. Added to their discomfort was the knowledge that they had lost all sense of direction. Hashknife knew they were travelling parallel to the river until they were shot at, and from that time on he wasn't sure of anything.

He felt they had travelled more than a mile, but they found no wagon-road. There were no stars to guide them, and the wind had shifted several times.

"'We're lost, the captain shouted,'" declared Sleepy, as they halted against the bank of a washout, where the wind and rain did not strike them so heavily.

"That wind was blowin' from the north when we started, and we tried to foller the wind," laughed Hashknife. "Is yore tobacco wet?"

They rolled a smoke and considered things.

"I wish we was back in that nice warm caboose," said Sleepy. "Gosh, that shore was a comfortable place. But this is jist my luck. It makes five times we've started East with a train of cows—and never got out of the sagebrush."

"Aw, we'll pick 'em up in Pinnacle City, Sleepy."

"Yeah, that's great. But where's Pinnacle City?"

"Two miles from the railroad bridge."

"Good guesser."

"It can't be more than nine o'clock, Sleepy. By golly, there ought to be somebody livin' in this place-where-the-wind-comes-from."

"If they're all like that jigger we ran into back there, I don't care about meetin' 'em," declared Sleepy. "Anyway, the tooth has quit hurtin'. I think the swellin' busted when we stopped at the bridge. That engineer shore knows how to spike his mount's tail to the earth!"

"There's only three things that are botherin' me," said Hashknife. "One is: Why did that party take a shot at us? And the other two are my boots full of water."

"And there's another small matter," said Sleepy, flapping his arms dismally. "We ain't taken any nourishment since this mornin', Hashknife."

"Yeah, there's that small matter," agreed Hashknife. "Oh, if yuh ever stop to check up on things, Sleepy, the world is all wrong. But never stop grinnin' and look back. The only place yuh ever see ghosts is behind yuh."

"Well, that wasn't no ghost that snapped his gun at us."

"He shore wasn't, cowboy. That jigger was plumb alive. Well, I dunno but what we might as well keep circlin'. Eventually we'll wear a trail, if we keep goin' long enough. I wish I knew which was south."

They sloshed away from the brush and headed down a slope.

"There's a light!" exclaimed Sleepy. "Straight ahead."

A flurry of rain obliterated the light, but it flickered again.

"Light in a winder," said Sleepy. "Must be a house."

"Must be," agreed Hashknife dryly. "Windows don't usually occur without a house in connection."

They struck a corral fence, followed it around to the stable and then headed for the house. It was the HJ ranch. But these two cowboys were far too wise to walk right up to a strange house in the dark, especially after having been shot at so recently; so they sidled up to the house and took a look through the window.

It was a side window of the living-room, and in the room were Peggy Wheeler, Laura Hatton and Honey Bee. It was evident to Hashknife and Sleepy that the living-room roof had sprung a leak and the three people were making an earnest endeavour to catch the water in a wash-tub, dish-pan and numerous other receptacles.

A long dry period had warped the old shingles of the ranch-house to such an extent that they leaked like a sieve.

"Looks like a harmless place," observed Hashknife.

"And not a heap of a lot of advantage over bein' outside," said Sleepy. "Any way, they look awful human."

They walked around to the front door, clumped up the steps and knocked on the door. Honey Bee answered the knock by opening the door about six inches and peering out.

"We just wondered if yuh didn't need a couple of good men to fix yore roof," said Hashknife seriously.

Honey opened the door a little and peered out at them. He had never seen either of them before, but the lamplight illuminated their faces enough to show their grins.

"Fix the roof?" he said slowly. "Oh, yeah. Well, I'll bet we do need help."

He opened the door.

"C'mon in out of the wet."

They shuffled the mud off their boots and came in. The two girls stood near the dining-room doorway, each of them holding a receptacle, looking curiously at Hashknife, who removed his dripping hat and grinned widely at them. Hashknife's grin was irresistible. Honey grinned foolishly and shuffled his feet.

"My name's Hartley," said Hashknife. "This soakin' wet object with me is named Stevens. He was sufferin' from a bad tooth, and we went huntin' a dentist in the rain."

"Yuh went huntin' a dentist?" queried Honey foolishly. "Wh-where didja expect to find one?"

"Sounds kinda queer," grinned Hashknife. "Yuh see, we was actin' as a couple of chambermaids to a train of cows, but the bridge caught on fire and we got stalled. Sleepy's tooth shore needed help; so we started out to find the wagon-bridge, figurin' to find this Pinnacle City. But we didn't find the bridge."

"Oh, yeah," Honey scratched his head. "The railroad bridge caught fire. Uh-huh. Ho-o-o-old on!"

He ran across the room, grabbed up a washbasin and placed it under a fresh leak. Then he came back and introduced the girls to Hashknife and Sleepy.

"My name's Bee," he said. "B-e-e."

"Last or first?" asked Hashknife.

"Last. Say, I better rustle some wood for that fireplace. Kinda take the chill off the air. Gosh, you fellers shore are wet."

Honey hurried away for some wood, while Hashknife moved some of the containers to more advantageous spots. There seemed to be no end to the leaks in the HJ ranch-house.

"Terrible, isn't it?" smiled Peggy.

It seemed to her that these two strange cowboys, even with their wet garments and muddy boots, had brought a warmth and cheer to the ranch that was sorely needed.

"Oh, not so bad," said Hashknife, squinting at a leak. "Didja ever stop to think how much worse it would be if them few little spots were the only place where it didn't leak?"

"That would be terrible," declared Laura.

"Yeah, it would. But suppose it leaked everywhere. That would be worse, eh?"

"Do you always look at things that way?" asked Peggy.

"Mostly," said Hashknife seriously. "Why not, Miss Wheeler? Sunlight is brighter than shadows; and it's a lot easier to find, if yuh look for it. Bright things are easier to see than dark ones."

"You listen to him a while and he'll prove to yuh that a leaky roof is a godsend," laughed Sleepy.

"Well, ain't it?" asked Hashknife. "If this roof hadn't leaked, you folks would probably have been in bed—and we wouldn't have seen their light, Sleepy."

"That is true," said Laura. "Oh, it was way past bedtime at the HJ ranch!"

Honey came in with an armful of wood, which he threw in the big fireplace.

"I'm makin' a bet you fellers are hungry," he said.

"Never mind that," grinned Hashknife. "Point us the way to Pinnacle City, and we'll be on our way."

"Not in that rain," declared Peggy quickly.

She went into the kitchen, where she called Wong Lee.

"Aw, don't bother the cook," begged Hashknife. "Pshaw, it ain't worth it."

"It's no bother to Wong Lee," said Peggy. "You boys get over by that fire and dry out a little. Wong Lee will get you a meal, and Honey will show you where to sleep. Laura and I will go to bed. Good-night, everybody."

"Good-night, and thank yuh a thousand times."

Hashknife and Sleepy crossed the room and shook hands with the two girls. Peggy smiled at Hashknife.

"Thank you for coming," she said.

The two cowboys went back to the fire and removed some of their wet garments, after which Hashknife went back to the porch and got their waterproof war-bags, which contained some dry clothing. They could hear Wong Lee shuffling about the kitchen, preparing them a meal.

He came to the door and looked in on them. He was a little, wizen-faced Celestial.

"Yo' like some ham-egg?" he asked.

Hashknife grinned at him, but did not reply. A smile slowly stole across the Chinaman's face and he bobbed his head.

"Yessa, velly good," he said. "No tlouble."

"You kinda got the Injun sign on Wong Lee," grunted Honey. "Darned old rascal almost laughed. I tell yuh, he ain't even smiled since Jim Wheeler was killed."

"Thasso?" Hashknife borrowed Sleepy's tobacco and rolled a cigarette. "What happened to Jim Wheeler?"

"Horse dragged him to death the other day."

Hashknife shuddered. The thought of a man's hanging by one foot to a stirrup never failed to rasp his nerves. He had seen men die that way, and once when he was but a youngster he had been thrown from a wild horse and had hung from a stirrup. Luckily the horse had whirled into a fence corner, where another cowboy was able to hold the animal and extricate Hashknife.

"Tough way to die," said Hashknife.

"Y'betcha," nodded Honey. "Head all busted up on the rocks, and his leg twisted. Golly, it shore was awful! He owned this HJ outfit. I work for the Flyin' H, but I'm down here kinda helpin' out. Hozie, Jim's brother, owns the Flyin' H."

"Miss Wheeler is Jim's daughter, eh?"

"Uh-huh. It's shore been a hard time for her, Hartley," Honey lowered his voice. "She was engaged to marry Joe Rich, and he got drunk on his weddin' night. Didn't show up. Then Peggy aims to go East with Laura Hatton. Yuh see, Jim wasn't awful well heeled with money. He owes the Pinnacle bank quite a lot; so he borrows five thousand from Ed Merrick, who owns the Circle M, and gives Ed his note.

"Ed gives him the money, and Jim starts home with it. And that's the last anybody ever seen of the money. Joe Rich was aimin' to pull out of the country; so he comes out to tell Peggy good-bye. And Joe was the one who found Jim Wheeler. Hozie Wheeler and Lonnie Myers comes ridin' along just a little later, and found Joe with Jim.

"And when the sheriff finds out about the missin' money, he tries to make Joe wait for an investigation, and Joe pops him through the gun arm. That's the last we saw of Joe. There's a reward for him, and the sheriff has been ridin' the hocks off his horse, but ain't found nothin'. So yuh can see it's been awful tough for Peggy."

Hashknife had been standing on one foot like a stork, holding the other foot out to the blazing fire, while Honey sketched his story. Sleepy hunched down, his back to the fire, his damp hair straggling down over his forehead.

"I wonder," he said, "if it ain't stopped rainin' enough for us to go on to town? We don't want to miss that train, Hashknife."

"Joe Rich was the sheriff," said Honey, as an afterthought. "But he resigned the mornin' after he got drunk. They made a sheriff out of his deputy. Jim Wheeler knocked Joe down that mornin', but Joe didn't do anythin', they say."

"And it hadn't ought to take long to fix that bridge," said Sleepy. "This rain would put the fire out."

"What kind of a jigger was this Joe Rich?" asked Hashknife curiously.

"Jist salt of the earth, Hartley."

"Uh-huh," thoughtfully. "And got so drunk he forgot to get married, eh?"

"Yeah, that's true," sighed Honey. "I dunno why he did; and he never said."

"Didn't have no quarrel with the girl?"

"Oh, no! Aw, it was to be a big marriage. I was to be best man. I almost crippled myself for life, tryin' to wear number six shoes."

"You come eat now?" asked Wong Lee.

Honey sat down with them. Sleepy looked gloomily at Hashknife and reminded him gently that sugar was for the coffee, and not for the eggs.

Hashknife chuckled, but sobered quickly. The rain still pattered on the old roof and dripped off the eaves. It was warm in the kitchen.

"Five thousand dollars is a lot of money," mused Hashknife, stirring his coffee with a fork. He had used the same fork to dip sugar from the bowl and did not seem to realise that it had all leaked out.

Sleepy knew the symptoms and groaned inwardly. Years of association with Hashknife had taught Sleepy to recognise the sudden moods of the tall cowboy. Trouble and mystery affected Hashknife as the scent of upland fowl affects a pointer.

Hashknife, in the days of his callow youth, had been known as George. His father, an itinerant minister in the Milk River country and head of a big family, had had little time or money to do more than just let this boy grow up. As soon as he was able to sit in a saddle he lived with the cowboys and became one of them.

Blessed with a balanced mind, possibly inherited from his father, who surely needed a balanced mind to make both ends meet, the boy struck out for himself, absorbing all kinds of knowledge, studying human nature. Eventually he drifted to the ranch, which gave him his nickname, and here he met the grinning Sleepy Stevens, whose baptismal name was David.

From the Hashknife ranch their trail led to many places. Soldiers of fortune they became, although Hashknife referred to themselves as cowpunchers of disaster. From the wide lands of Alberta to the Mexican Border they had left their mark. They did not stay long in any place, unless fate decreed that a certain time must elapse before their work was finished. And then they would go on, possibly poorer in pocket. Their life had made them fatalists, had made them very human. To salve their own consciences they declared that they were looking for the right spot to settle down; a place to live out the rest of their life in peaceable pursuits.

But down in their hearts they knew that this place did not exist. They wanted to see the other side of the hill. Hashknife's brain rebelled against a mystery. It seemed to challenge him to combat. Where range detectives had failed utterly because they were unable to see beyond actual facts, Hashknife's analytical mind had enabled him to build up chains of evidence that had cleared up mystery after mystery.

But solving mysteries was not a business with them. They did not pose as detectives. It merely happened that fate threw them into contact with these things. Sleepy's mind did not function with any more rapidity than that of any average man, but he was blessed with a vast sense of humour, bull-dog tenacity and a faculty for using a gun when a gun was most needed.

Whether it was merely a pose or not, Sleepy always tried to prevent Hashknife from getting interested in these mysteries of the range country. He argued often and loud, but to no avail. But once started, Sleepy worked as diligently as Hashknife. Neither of them were wizards with their guns. No amount of persuasion would induce them to compete with others in marksmanship, nor did they ever practise drawing a gun.

"Leave that to the gun-men," Hashknife had said. "We're not gun-men."

Which was something that many men would take great pains to disprove, along the back-trail of Hashknife and Sleepy.

And right now, while he ate heavily of the HJ food, Sleepy Stevens knew he was being dragged into the whirlpool of the Tumbling River range. He could tell by the twitch of Hashknife's nose, by the calculating squint of his gray eyes; and if that was not enough—Hashknife was cutting a biscuit with a knife and fork.

"Five thousand is a lot of money for the HJ to lose," agreed Honey. "Take that along with the seven thousand owin' to the Pinnacle City bank and it jist about nails the HJ to the floor and leaves it there to starve."

"Was Jim Wheeler a sickly man?" asked Hashknife.

"Sickly? Not a bit; he was built like a bull."

"Drink much?"

"Hardly ever took a drink."

"Ride a bad horse?"

"Been ridin' the same one three years, and it never made a bobble. Jim's bronc-scratchin' days was over, Hartley."

"Uh-huh," Hashknife rubbed his chin with the fork. "Was it goin' to take five thousand dollars for to ship that girl back East?"

"Probably not."

"What kind of a feller is Ed Merrick?"

"Good cow-man. He's one of the county commissioners. Owned the Circle M about five years, and is kind of a big man in the county. Mostly horse outfit."

"Yuh say they made a sheriff out of the deputy?"

"Yeah; Len Kelsey."

Honey described the trouble on the street between Kelsey and Rich, in which Kelsey was wounded. He also told them how the cowboys hid out to keep from being sworn in to follow the fugitive. This interested Sleepy.

"Sounds like there was some reg'lar boys around here," he said.

"Oh, the boys like Joe," grinned Honey. "You'd like him."

"I dunno. Any man that ain't got no more sense than to get drunk and miss a chance of a wife like that dark-haired girl ain't very much of a feller. Or the blonde one."

"The blonde one is my girl," said Honey softly.

Sleepy reached impulsively across the table and shook hands with Honey, who looked foolish.

"I'm glad yuh told me," said Sleepy seriously. "Prob'ly save me a lot of heartaches. She's a dinger."

Hashknife shoved back from the table, thanking Wong Lee for his hospitality.

"Velly good," Wong Lee bobbed his head. "No tlouble. You come some mo'."

"Mebbe we will, Wong."

"All lite; I cook plenty."

The rain had increased again, and Honey advised them against attempting to go to Pinnacle City. It was not difficult to convince them. Sleepy's tooth did not ache any more, and their clothes were beginning to dry; so they followed Honey down to the dry bunk-house and went to bed.

It did not take the rain long to extinguish the fire at the bridge, and after an examination the train crews decided that it was still safe. Many of the timbers were badly charred, and but for the heavy rain which followed the wind, the whole bridge would have been doomed.

The cattle-train, minus two of the cowhands, proceeded slowly to Pinnacle City, where it took the siding. It would spend several hours there, watering stock, and the man in charge expected Hashknife and Sleepy to put in an appearance before leaving time.

The passenger train drew in at the station, possibly an hour late. The wires being down, it was impossible for them to get orders. The heavy rain swept the wooden platform, but the depot agent trundled out some express packages. The express car door was partly open, but there was no messenger.

The agent climbed into the car, and the first thing that greeted his eye was the through safe, almost in the centre of the car, its door torn open. A single car light burned in the upper end of the car, and it was there that the agent found the messenger, bound hand and foot.

Running back to the depot, the agent told what he had found, and the train crew hurried to the car, while another man went to get an officer. In the waiting room of the depot the express messenger told what he knew of the robbery. A man had struck him over the head, and he was a trifle hazy about what had happened.

The man had boarded the car at Kelo. The messenger said he had received several packages from the agent at Kelo, and had gone to place them before closing the door. The wind was blowing a gale, and he did not hear the man come in. In fact he merely surmised that the man got on at Kelo, because as far as he knew there was no other man than himself on the car when they stopped at Kelo.

At any rate the man had forced him at the point of a revolver to close and lock the door, and had made him sit down and wait for the train to pull out. There was quite a long delay, and the bandit seemed rather nervous.

In fact he grew so nervous that he knocked the messenger unconscious with his gun, and the messenger didn't know that the safe had been blown open. He dimly remembered a loud noise, but was in no shape to find out what it was. Anyway, the robber had bound and placed him behind some trunks out of the way of the explosion.

He was just a little sick all over, yet he gave Len Kelsey a fairly good description of the robber—as good as usually is given. A masked man of medium height. Might have been tall, or possibly short. Wore black sombrero, striped shirt, overalls and boots. No vest. The shirt might have been blue and white—or red and green. The messenger wasn't sure. He noted particularly that the robber had a six-shooter in his right hand, and that he wore leather cuffs—black leather, with silver stars in a circle around the upper edge of the cuffs.

"Was there any money in the safe?" asked Len.

"A lot of it," declared the messenger. "I don't know how much. I'd like to see a doctor about my head."

Slim Coleman, of the Lazy B, happened to be there at the depot, and he walked back with Len Kelsey.

"What do yuh think about it, Len?" he asked.

"I dunno," lied Len.

Slim had noted the expression of Len's face when the messenger told about the leather cuffs.

When Joe Rich had left Pinnacle City he was wearing a blue and white striped shirt, black sombrero, overalls and a pair of black leather cuffs, on which were riveted a lot of small, silver stars. Joe had done the decorating himself, and Slim knew that no other cowboy in the Tumbling River country wore a cuff like Joe's.

Len did not seem inclined to talk about it so Slim went back to the depot, where old Doctor Curzon was bandaging up the messenger's head. A drink of raw liquor had helped to make the messenger more sociable and willing to talk.

"You got a good look at his gun, didn't yuh?" asked Slim.

"I felt it," smiled the messenger, wincing slightly from Doctor Curzon's ministrations.

"What did it look like?"

"Very large calibre—about six inches in diameter." The man laughed at his description. "Weighed a ton. Seriously, I can't describe it, but it seems to me that it had a white handle. Perhaps it was yellow, like bone. You know what I mean—not pearl. It was a Colt, I am sure."

Slim sighed deeply.

"Man wear any rings on his fingers?"

"I didn't see any."

Slim went back uptown. Joe Rich carried a Colt .45 with a yellow bone handle. Slim remembered when Joe had carved out those pieces of bone, working for days, at odd times, shaping the grip to fit his hand. Slim didn't know of another cowpuncher in the country that carried a bone-handled gun.

The news spread quickly around the town that the safe of the passenger train had been blown by a lone bandit who wore silver stars on his cuffs and carried a bone-handled gun. Joe Rich's name did not need to be mentioned. Len Kelsey did nothing, because there was nothing to be done. The telegraph wires were down and there was no use of his riding out into the storm. Even if the robber did get out at the river bridge, the storm would wipe out any tracks he might make, and even if there were no storm, how could he track one man?

Len Kelsey was very wise. He stayed at home where it was warm and dry, and went to bed. He had sufficient description to prove who had pulled the job, and he had already worn out two perfectly good horses trying to find this elusive young man.

CHAPTER VI:
HASHKNIFE SMELLS A RAT

Sometime during that night the trouble shooters for the telegraph company had repaired the break and this enabled the despatchers to straighten out the trains. The cattle-train headed out of Pinnacle City the following morning, minus two cowboys.

The depot agent knew about this, and told Len Kelsey that there were two lost cowpunchers somewhere on the east side of the river. The agent knew from what he had heard the crew of the cattle-train say that these men had left the train, intending to walk down to the wagon-bridge. But he also knew they had taken their war-bags with them and had buckled on their belts and guns before leaving the train.

"Kinda looks as though they intended missin' the train," said Kelsey.

"Might be worth investigating, Sheriff. The passenger was close behind the cattle-train for a long time out there by the bridge. And that express messenger had been hit so hard on the head that he wasn't sure of anything."

"Sure—I'll look into it," agreed Len. "I won't leave any stone unturned."

He had read this in a book, and it sounded like the proper thing for a sheriff to say.

Hashknife and Sleepy did not mention to Peggy that Honey Bee had told them about her troubles. She was in good spirits that morning, and even Wong Lee sang at his work. Laura told Honey that Peggy had talked quite a while about the tall cowboy and his wonderful grin—and Honey told Hashknife about it.

"Didn't either of 'em mention me?" asked Sleepy. "No? That's tough. But how could I grin, with my jaw all swelled? But that's jist my luck!"

Honey offered to take them to Pinnacle City in the buggy. They were hitching up the horses when Len Kelsey and Jack Ralston rode in.

"Now, what do them whip-poor-wills want?" growled Honey. "That's the sheriff and deputy."

"What had we ought to do—put up our hands?" asked Sleepy.

The two officers dismounted and spoke to Honey.

"Howdy," growled Honey.

Hashknife could plainly see that Honey Bee did not care for these two officers of the law.

Len Kelsey studied Hashknife and Sleepy for a moment.

"I reckon you boys are the two missin' members of the cattle-train outfit, eh?"

"If there's two missin'—we're both of 'em," said Hashknife gravely. "Has the train left Pinnacle City?"

"Before daylight."

"Stranded again," groaned Sleepy. "I'll never see the East, that's a cinch."

Hashknife hitched up his belt and leaned against the buggy.

"Yuh wasn't exactly lookin' for us, was yuh?" he asked.

"I don't hardly think so," replied Kelsey. "The safe on the express car of the passenger train that stopped back of yuh at the bridge last night was dynamited somewhere between Kelo and Pinnacle City."

Hashknife and Sleepy exchanged a quick glance. That might explain why a shot had been fired at them in the dark. They had blundered into the bandit, who was making his getaway.

"For gosh sake!" snorted Honey. "Did they get much, Len?"

"Dunno how much. One man pulled the job, Honey—a man who wore black leather cuffs with silver stars, and a bone-handled six-shooter."

"Leather cuffs with silver stars and bone—" Honey stopped and came in closer to the sheriff.

"Are yuh sure of that, Len?"

"That's the messenger's description."

"Well, for gosh sake!"

Honey looked toward the house, shaking his head sadly.

"You recognise the description?" asked Hashknife.

"Joe Rich," said Honey. "He made the stars and put 'em on a pair of black cuffs and he made the bone handles for his gun. Yuh say yuh don't know how much he got, Len?"

"No, I don't, Honey. But it was enough, I reckon."

"Uh-huh. Excuse me, I forgot to introduce you gents."

After the introduction they all sat down on the steps of the bunk-house and rolled smokes. Hashknife did not tell the sheriff about the shot that was fired at them in the dark.

"I dunno just where to start," admitted Kelsey. "I've been huntin' Joe Rich all over these hills, and now he comes back and robs a train right under my nose."

Kelsey, who was still wearing his arm in a sling, noticed Hashknife looking at it.

"A little souvenir of makin' a fool move," he said.

"Yeah, I heard about it," nodded Hashknife. "Joe Rich must be pretty fast with a gun, eh?"

"Fast enough," growled Kelsey. "Funny, ain't it? Here I was his deputy all this time, and now I'm huntin' him. Don't seem right."

"Are yuh dead sure it is?" asked Hashknife seriously.

Kelsey looked quickly at him.

"Dead sure?" Kelsey laughed shortly. "Well about as sure as anythin' could be, Hartley. I dunno what got into Joe. He was sure strong on enforcin' the law, and now he seems just as strong on breakin' it."

"Them's the kind that go wrong—when they do go," said Ralston.

"Yeah, you know a lot about it!" snorted Honey.

"Well, it allus works out that way."

"It does, eh? I suppose yuh knowed two months ago that Joe Rich would turn out bad. What do yuh use—palmistry or one of them glass balls?"

"Aw, yuh don't need to get sore, Honey."

"Thasso? Every time I think about Joe, I get sore. I wish I knowed where he was hidin' out."

"Me, too," grinned Kelsey. "I'd be a thousand better off."

"Yea-a-a-ah? Well, when you find out where he is, yuh better take plenty of help along to get him, Len; two of yuh ain't enough."

Kelsey could see that the argument might wax rather hot; so he got to his feet, stretched wearily and told Ralston they better be going. Nobody asked them to stay. Honey looked after them morosely.

"Don't like 'em, eh?" queried Hashknife.

"No! You boys go ahead and hitch up the team. I've got to tell the girls about that robbery. I sure hate to tell Peggy that they think Joe pulled that job, but I'd rather tell her than to have her get it from somebody else."

The team was hitched when Honey came back, and he drove out to the main road.

"How did she take it?" asked Hashknife.

Honey looked at Hashknife, a pained expression on his face.

"A-a-a-aw heck!" he said explosively.

"Does she believe it?"

"Huh! I dunno what she believes. Yuh can't tell nothin' about a woman, Hartley. She didn't say anythin'. I was wonderin' if she heard what I told her, but I reckon she did. Anyway she didn't say anythin'—jist walked away."

They jolted along over the rough road. Honey turned to Hashknife, a grin on his lips.

"I ain't no gentleman," he said.

"Ain't yuh?" asked Hashknife.

"Nossir," Honey shook his head violently. "Can't lie good enough. Laura said I ought to be crowned with an axe-handle for comin' in and tellin' Peggy that Joe Rich robbed the train. She said I should have lied about it."

"Mebbe yuh should."

"Cinch! Giddap! I always think of a lie too late. Some day I'm goin' to be hung for tellin' the truth."

"You'll be the first puncher that ever had that honour," said Sleepy. "There's that bridge we was huntin' for, Hashknife. If we'd 'a' found it last night, we'd be on our way East right now."

"Glad yuh didn't," grinned Honey, as they rattled over the loose floor-planks of the bridge. "It's only a little ways out here to where Jim Wheeler was killed. I'll show yuh the place."

He drove off the bridge and around to the spot where Joe had found Jim Wheeler. Honey knew the exact spot and drew just off the road. Hashknife walked up and down the road while Honey explained things to him. The rain of the night before had laid the dust, and the road was almost as smooth as asphalt.

After looking the place over they rode on to Pinnacle City, where they met Uncle Hozie Wheeler and Aunt Emma. Honey introduced them to Hashknife and Sleepy, and told how they happened to be in the Tumbling River country.

They had heard about the train robbery. It seemed to be the general opinion that Joe Rich had done it.

"I knowed him a long time," said Uncle Hozie. "He never struck me as bein' a bad boy in any way. I don't *sabe* him. Why, he jist went all to bits in a week!"

"Does Peggy know about it?" asked Aunt Emma.

"Yeah," Honey nodded solemnly. "Yeah, she knows. But I've told her the last bad news I'll ever tell."

"Took it hard, did she, Honey?"

"I dunno. She never said anythin'. Laura gave me hell. Sometimes I think that girl don't care for the truth. Oh, if she wants lies, I reckon I can supply her."

Uncle Hozie and Aunt Emma were going to ride out to the HJ to see the girls. Curt Bellew and Ed Merrick were at the Pinnacle. They shook hands with Honey, who introduced Hashknife and Sleepy.

"What do yuh think of Joe Rich now?" asked Curt, after he had invited them to share his hospitality.

"Jist the same as I always did," declared Honey. "Somethin' has gone wrong with the boy. How's the Circle M, Merrick?"

"All right, Honey. I'll bet yore old ranch-house leaked last night."

"Did it? My gosh, I'll betcha it did. Ask Hartley and Stevens; they showed up in the rain. Yuh see, they was on that stalled cow-train, and Stevens had a toothache; so they tried to find their way to the wagon-bridge in order to get to town. But I reckon they got kinda lost, and ended up at the HJ."

Merrick laughed.

"I don't believe I could have found my way either—as well as I know the country. Whew! It sure was dark and wet. My place didn't leak, but it got damp. Are you boys goin' to be with us a while?"

"I dunno," Hashknife leaned an elbow on the bar and began rolling a cigarette. "It looks as though Fate kinda dropped us off here for some reason or other."

"Too bad it's the slack season. I'm short two men of my regular crew, but there ain't enough work for me and Ben Collins and 'Dutch' Seibert. Later on I might use yuh."

"I loaned Honey to the HJ," laughed Bellew. "I've still got Eph Harper and Slim Coleman on my hands. Ma says that's two men too many. She allus says

I'm tryin' to make a mountain out of a mole-hill—meanin' that I can't ever hire enough men to make the Lazy B a big cow outfit."

While they were drinking a man came in whom the bartender seemed to know. It was the telegraph operator at the depot. He bought a drink and a cigar.

"I suppose the sheriff is hunting bandits," he said.

"We seen him out at the HJ this mornin'," offered Honey.

The man nodded.

"I was just over to his office, but there was anybody home. Had a telegram from him for Ransome. They found a little gold pen-knife in the express car. It didn't belong to the messenger, he said. The wire said there were the initials J.R. on the handle."

"J.R.?" said Honey. "Little gold knife! My gosh, that's the knife Peggy gave Joe for his birthday!"

"I dunno," said the man vacantly. "All I know is what the wire said. I reckon it will keep until the sheriff gets back."

He went out, and Merrick laughed softly.

"He guesses it will keep. Ha, ha, ha, ha!"

Honey leaned on the bar and looked dismally at himself in the mirror.

"I'll not tell Peggy," he declared, but amended it with, "I might come right out and tell her that if anybody says they found Joe Rich's gold knife on that car—they lie."

"Why even mention it?" asked Hashknife.

"Mebbe that's the best thing to do. Oh, they've got Joe cinched!"

"But he overlooked one bet," said Hashknife thoughtfully.

"What was that?" asked Merrick.

"He forgot to carve his name on the safe."

"Is that meant to be serious?" asked Merrick.

"No-o-o-o," drawled Hashknife. "I suppose I'm jokin'."

"Aw, he wouldn't write his name on the safe," said Honey.

"Might as well," grinned Hashknife. "It sure shows that Joe is a beginner at the game. A regular hold-up man don't tag his work thataway."

Merrick looked seriously at Hashknife. "You talk as though you were familiar with hold-up men, Hartley."

"No; I just use common sense, Merrick."

"Uh-huh. Well, it's a good thing to use. A lot of us don't do it."

"No, that's true," admitted Hashknife seriously.

Merrick scratched his chin and turned back to the bar. He wasn't exactly sure whether this tall, level-eyed cowboy was making fun of him or not. He had the feeling that he was, but there was nothing to justify this feeling. Both of the strange cowboys were very serious of face, and Sleepy's blue eyes looked entirely innocent. But Merrick did not know that Sleepy's innocent blue eyes were his greatest asset.

"I wonder if the sheriff's office had anythin' to go on this mornin'," said Merrick.

"Couple of horses," replied Sleepy. "Now let me buy a drink, will yuh?"

"I've got to go kinda easy," said Curt Bellew. "I git down here and lap up liquor, and have to eat cloves all the way back to the ranch."

"And then prove why yuh ate cloves," grinned Honey.

"Sure. Honey, if yo're a wise boy, you'll stay sober and single."

"A-a-aw, I don't drink much, Curt."

"Yuh don't get married much either, do yuh?"

"Well," laughed Honey, "I won't get drunk and forget to get married."

Bellew and Merrick left the saloon and a few minutes later Honey, Hashknife and Sleepy stocked up on tobacco and rode back to the HJ.

"I feel foolish goin' back there," said Hashknife. "Kinda looks as though we were imposin' on yuh."

"Yuh throw that in a can," said Honey. "Yo're welcome to stay as long as yuh can. I can't quite *sabe* you two boys."

"Jist in what way?"

"Well, I never seen yuh before until last night. Yuh come in and I forget that I don't know yuh. I tell yuh all about the trouble, and—well, yuh know what I mean, don'tcha? It jist seemed the natural thing to do. And Wong Lee took to yuh. Wong's kinda funny thataway.

"Why, sometimes the boys from the Circle M stop here. Yuh see they go past here to their ranch from town. Wong ain't never spoken to one of 'em. Other fellers show up here at mealtime, and Wong says nothin'. But he shore talked to yuh, and promised yuh more meals. Do dogs ever foller yuh?"

"Sometimes," laughed Hashknife.

"I'll betcha. Never bite yuh, do they?"

"Haven't yet."

"Never will. Huh!" Honey jerked up on the lines. "I know what the word is. I read somethin' about it in a magazine. It's called personality. Know what it means, Hartley?"

"Yeah, I think I do."

"Well, that's what you've got. Giddap, broncs! Joe Rich had it. His must 'a' back-fired on him."

Hashknife laughed. Honey Bee was so sincere in his statements.

"Was Rich a good sheriff?" asked Hashknife.

"Y'betcha. Joe was a man that wouldn't stop at anythin' to enforce the law. Some men kinda play fav'rites, yuh know. But Joe wasn't that kind. At least I don't reckon he was, and I knew him awful well."

"How did it happen that you wasn't his deputy?"

"Politics," explained Honey. "Merrick controls a lot of votes in this county, and he told Joe he'd support him if he'd appoint Len Kelsey deputy. Joe agreed, and it was the Merrick vote that won for Joe."

"Who was the other candidate?"

"John Leeds, of Ransome. He's a hard old customer, Hartley. He was sheriff before Joe was elected, and he made a lot of enemies. Pretty smart, too. I'll betcha, if old John was sheriff he'd 'a' been on the trail of that robber before daylight. He was a sticker, old John was, and nobody ever told him what to do. Mebbe that's why he got beat."

They drove along to where Jim Wheeler had been killed, and Hashknife leaned out of the buggy. But he did not say anything. They drove across the bridge and to the HJ, where they saw the Flying H buggy team tied to the front porch.

"Uncle Hozie and Aunt Emma," said Honey. "They're salt of the earth, gents. Always tryin' to do somethin' for yuh. Aunt Emma hops all over yuh for doin' somethin', but all the time she's laughin' inside at yuh. They don't make 'em any better. Hozie and Jim was pretty thick, and it hurt Hozie to see old Jim pass out. He didn't say much—but that's his way. Tears don't show much—except moisture."

Hashknife and Sleepy went to the bunk-house, and did not see Uncle Hozie and his wife until they were ready to drive away. Honey had told them about the gold-handled knife, but did not tell Peggy. A little later Ed Merrick stopped on his way out to the Circle M and talked with the three cowboys about the robbery of the night before. He was expecting a horse buyer from Kelo, so did not linger long.

"How are prices in this range?" asked Hashknife.

"Depends on the buyer," replied Merrick. "Some of 'em play square with yuh. The horse market ain't very strong, and we have to almost take what's offered. This buyer wants quite a lot of horses, so he says."

"For Eastern market?"

"Yeah, I think so. Anyway, the buyer is from the East."

Merrick rode away and a few minutes later Wong Lee rang the dinner bell. Peggy and Laura did not eat with the boys, but a little later Hashknife wandered around the rear of the house and found Peggy sitting on an old bench in the shade of the cotton woods, a picture of abject lonesomeness.

Hashknife squatted down on his heels against the tree and rolled a cigarette. Neither of them had spoken. Peggy sighed and leaned against the bole of the tree, watching Hashknife's long lean fingers fashion a cigarette.

"My, it's shore peaceful out here!" said Hashknife.

Peggy nodded slowly.

"Yes, it is peaceful."

"It kinda looks as though we were imposin' on yuh."

"You are not," declared Peggy quickly. "I'm glad you came. And I don't know why I'm glad. Queer, isn't it?"

"Yeah, it's queer. Life's a queer thing. Yesterday we were on our way East in that caboose, when the bridge caught fire and changed everythin'. Yuh never know what will come tomorrow."

"I realise that, Mr. Hartley. I suppose Honey has told you of the things that have happened lately."

"Well, yeah, I reckon we've heard quite a lot about it, ma'am. It shore was tough luck. Are yuh goin' away with Miss Hatton?"

"No; I can't."

"Uh-huh."

"Oh, it doesn't matter," she said wearily. "You see, I've got to stay and see that things are straightened up. Dad owed the bank seven thousand. Oh, I wish he had let things go as they were! I didn't need that trip. He was so thoughtful of me, and he thought I'd like to get away for a while. Now he's gone, and the ranch—we'll have to sell everything in order to pay the debts."

"That's shore tough. Miss Wheeler, I'd like to know more about Joe Rich. I don't like to be personal, but I'd like to get yore opinion of him."

"My opinion?" Peggy laughed bitterly. "I don't think it is worth much, Mr. Hartley."

"Yore honest opinion, I mean."

"My honest opinion?"

"Yeah. Yuh see we all have two opinions on things like that—the one we express and the one we hide."

"I—I think I know what you mean, Mr. Hartley."

"Fine. I wish you'd leave the mister off my name. All my friends call me Hashknife. When anybody says 'Mr. Hartley' I look around to see who they're speakin' to. Now, yuh jist go ahead and tell me about Joe Rich."

Peggy looked earnestly at Hashknife.

"Why should I? Why do you wish to know about Joe Rich—my opinion of him? Who are you, anyway?"

Hashknife studied his boot-toes for several moments, but finally looked up at her with a grin in his eyes.

"It's kinda queer," he admitted, "but I'm one of them funny folks who always asks questions. All my life I've asked a lot of questions, Miss Wheeler. Sometimes I find out things. I'm like the feller who said he made up his mind to kiss every pretty woman he met. Somebody said—

"'I'll bet you got whipped a lot of times,' and he said—

"'Well, yeah, I did, but I shore got a lot of kisses.'

"And that's the way with me—except that I was after answers instead of kisses."

Peggy laughed with him.

"But I don't see yet," she said, "what good will my opinion do you? What do you want to know about Joe Rich?"

"Well, it's like this, Miss Wheeler: Yore opinion of him will go quite a ways with me. If I was to come right out and ask yuh if yuh loved Joe Rich in spite of everythin' he's done to yuh—what would yuh say?"

Peggy turned her head away and rested her chin on her hand. After a space of time she shook her head.

"That isn't a fair question," she said softly.

"No, but yuh gave me a fair answer," said Hashknife. "I'd like to shake hands with yuh, Miss Wheeler."

Wonderingly she shook hands with him, and he smiled down at her, his gray eyes twinkling.

"But I—I didn't answer you," she said, choking slightly.

"Oh, yes yuh did, Peggy. I'm goin' to call yuh Peggy. If yuh can love him in spite of everythin' he's done, by golly, he's worth savin' for yuh."

"Worth saving?" Peggy got to her feet. "I don't quite understand. How can you save him?"

"I dunno exactly," Hashknife scratched his head, tilting his sombrero over one eye. "But there ain't nothin' that can't be done."

"But what could save him? Why, they're hunting for him now—offering a big reward."

The tears came into her eyes and she turned away. Hashknife patted her on the shoulder.

"Keep smilin'," he said softly. "Remember how it was here last night? All wind and rain, wasn't it? And today the sun is shinin' and the sky is blue. Life's like that, Peggy. The old sky gets pretty black and all clouded up, but the old sun is always on the job, and it breaks through eventually."

"It is wonderful to look at things in that way, Hashknife."

"I think so, Peggy. My old man was that way. He preached the gospel in bunk-houses and out on the range. But he didn't wear a long face and say long prayers. He said he wasn't trying to make folks fit to die—he was makin' 'em fit to live. And after all, that's the gospel. If yo're fit to live, yuh'll be fit to die. And when yo're fit to live yuh'll always see the sun behind the clouds."

Peggy smiled at him through her tears. "I'm glad you came here," she said simply, and went back to the house.

Hashknife sat down on the bench and rolled a fresh cigarette. Sleepy had been sitting on the bunk-house steps, but now he came up to Hashknife and sat down beside him.

"Well, what do yuh know, cowboy?" queried Sleepy.

"What do I know?" Hashknife grinned wistfully at his smoke. "I know I've bit off a darned big chew for one man to masticate."

"Yeah," nodded Sleepy, "yuh mostly always do, Hashknife."

"Uh-huh. Where's Honey?"

"Settin' on the front porch with Laura. By golly, if this keeps up I'm goin' to get me a squaw. You at one end of the place and Honey at the other. While Mister Stevens sets on the bunk-house steps all alone. And he's the best-lookin' man on the ranch, too."

"Who is—Honey?"

"Na-a-aw—Stevens! Honey's second."

"And I'm third," grinned Hashknife.

"Sure," said Sleepy. "Wong Lee don't count because he's a Chinaman."

"I'm glad one entry is scratched. There goes the sheriff and his hired hand."

Len Kelsey and Jack Ralston rode past, heading for the old bridge.

"Reckon they didn't have very good luck," observed Sleepy. "That must 'a' been Joe Rich we almost ran into in the rain. He was just making his getaway, eh?"

"Looks thataway, Sleepy. Mebbe we should 'a' told the sheriff about it."

"That wouldn't help him any; yuh can't foller horse tracks."

"No, yuh can't," agreed Hashknife, getting up. "I reckon we better go down and see how many ridin' rigs there are on this place, and pick out a horse."

"Yuh mean to stay here a while, Hashknife?"

"It ain't an unpleasant place, is it?"

"No-o-o, but—"

"Yuh didn't hope to catch that train, didja?"

"The cattle-train? Certainly not."

"Have yuh got any other place you'd like to go to?"

"No-o-o-o, I reckon not, Hashknife."

"Fine! Then yuh don't mind stayin' a day or so, eh?"

They looked seriously at each other for a moment and both grinned widely as they headed for the stable.

CHAPTER VII:
CITY *V.* RANGE

The following day William H. Cates, special investigator of the Wells-Fargo, came to Pinnacle City, and went into a lengthy session with Len Kelsey and Jack Ralston. Cates was a big, burly man with a square jaw and blue eyes. In fifteen minutes he knew as much as Kelsey did about the robbery and the life of Joe Rich.

Cates' questions were snappy and to the point. But what he learned was of little value to him. Cates was a city man, an ex-detective of San Francisco. He knew much more about pavements than he did about ranges, and he was not egotistical enough to expect much success in this case.

"The idea seems to be—get Joe Rich," he said.

"Yeah, that's the idea," agreed Kelsey, resting his heels on the desk. "But how are yuh goin' to get him, pardner?"

"We've been after him for days," grumbled Ralston.

"He got over twenty thousand that last haul," said the detective.

"My gosh, was there that much in the safe?" exploded Kelsey. "Whew!"

"That much, at least, Sheriff. The company are offering a reward of twenty-five hundred."

"I didn't know they carried that much," said Ralston.

"Well, they do. Sometimes more, sometimes less."

"Well, what do yuh propose doin'?" asked Kelsey.

"Keep looking for Joe Rich, I suppose. You say he's got a lot of friends around here?"

Kelsey nodded glumly, remembering how the cowboys had avoided riding after Joe.

"Yeah, yuh can't expect much help, Cates. They'll all spot yuh—and these cowpunchers can shore be clams."

"Oh, I'm not going out to hunt him," smiled Cates. "I'd be a fool to do that. When you boys can't find him—what could I do? I don't know this country. Why, I haven't been on a horse for fifteen years!"

"Nope," Cates sighed deeply. "This is no job for a man like me. What this needs is a man like Hashknife Hartley."

"Hashknife Hartley?"

Kelsey pricked up his ears and took his feet off the desk. Jack Ralston showed proper interest.

Cates nodded slowly as he bit the end off a cigar.

"Yes, he might do something with it. Ever hear of him?"

"What about him?" asked Kelsey quickly.

Cates smiled as he puffed his cigar.

"I never met him," he said slowly. "One of those sagebrush *Sherlocks*, I suppose. Maybe I hadn't ought to make fun of him—he did some good work for my company. Oh, I've heard a lot about what he has done. It's our business to keep track of all those things, you see. But some of it sounds rather mythical."

"Well, that's shore funny," said Kelsey. "There's a Hartley and Stevens out at the HJ ranch right now."

"Eh?" Cates stared at Kelsey. "Hashknife Hartley?"

"I dunno; name's Hartley."

"Stevens? Huh! Say, I believe he has a partner by that name. Wouldn't that be funny if it was Hashknife Hartley. How do you get out to that HJ ranch?"

"We can take yuh out, Cates."

"Fine. But how do they happen to be here?"

Kelsey told him about the burning bridge and the stalled cattle-train.

"But do yuh reckon they'll work on the case?" asked Jack Ralston.

"We can soon find out. I'm curious to see him. It may not be the same man, but we can soon find that out, too."

Kelsey obtained a buggy at the livery-stable, in which he and Cates rode out to the HJ, while Ralston followed them on horseback. But they did not find Hashknife and Sleepy at the ranch. Kelsey introduced Cates to the two girls and Cates found out that Hartley's name was Hashknife.

"They rode away this morning with Honey Bee," said Peggy. "No, I don't know where they were going, Mr. Kelsey, nor when they'll come back."

"I see," nodded Cates. "Well, would you mind telling Hartley that William Cates, of the Wells-Fargo, is in Pinnacle City and is anxious to see him?"

"Why, certainly I'll tell him," replied Peggy.

"Do you know him?"

Cates smiled and shook his head.

"Only by reputation. I happened to mention his name to the sheriff and found that he was here at your ranch. He will find me at the Pinnacle Hotel."

They rode back to the gate, where Ralston told Kelsey he was going out to the Circle M.

"I've got a pair of boots out there," explained Ralston. "And if I don't get 'em pretty soon, somebody'll be wearin' 'em."

Ralston spurred away, while Kelsey and Cates rode back to Pinnacle City.

In the meantime Hashknife, Sleepy and Honey were riding through the hills south of the HJ. Hashknife rode a tall roan horse and Jim Wheeler's saddle and Sleepy bestrode a Roman-nosed buckskin and a saddle which had been purchased for Peggy.

Honey led them out on a high pinnacle where they could look over a great part of the Tumbling River range. To the southwest, about a mile away, was the Circle M ranch, half-hidden in a clump of green trees. To the northwest was the Lazy B, three miles away, which Honey was able to locate definitely by a gash in the hills. They could follow the windings of Tumbling River for miles in each direction. To the east of them was the railroad, winding around through the hills.

They could see the ribbon of smoke from a passing train heading for Kelo. Far down on the wagon road they could see a lone rider heading for the Circle M. It was Jack Ralston, going after his boots, though they didn't know it.

"Is it possible to ford the river near the HJ?" asked Hashknife, as they turned to ride back.

"The old ford is about two hundred yards below the bridge," said Honey. "There's an old sand-bar. Some of the old road may be washed out by this time, but I reckon yuh could get across all right."

"Don'tcha like to cross on bridges?" grinned Sleepy.

"Oh, sure. But sometimes I get finicky."

They swung down off the hills and struck the road, which they followed back to the HJ. Peggy came down to the corral and delivered Cates' message to Hashknife. The tall cowboy did not change expression, but leaned one elbow against the corral fence, as she told him about the coming of Kelsey, Ralston and Cates to see him.

"He didn't know you were here," she explained. "But he mentioned your name, and Mr. Kelsey told him where he could find you."

"I don't reckon I know Mr. Cates, Peggy."

"He said you didn't, but he wants to see you."

"Oh, yeah. Thank yuh very much, Peggy. How are yuh feelin'?"

"Better."

"That's great. I hope Wong Lee won't throw me out for the appetite I've got tonight."

Peggy laughed and assured him that Wong Lee loved people who had big appetites. Honey was a trifle curious about what Cates wanted.

"Said he was a Wells-Fargo man, eh? Prob'ly a detective."

"Prob'ly," said Hashknife dryly, hanging up his saddle.

"Just about how in heck did he happen to mention you?" wondered Sleepy.

Hashknife did not reply, but Sleepy knew that he was just a trifle curious himself. But both of them realised that they had figured in deals which affected the Wells-Fargo, and it would not be at all strange if an express company investigator had heard of them.

But they did not go to Pinnacle City that night. Hashknife did not seem at all interested in finding Mr. Cates, and Sleepy knew Hashknife too well to insist that they go to town. But Cates was not to be denied a chance to talk with Hashknife. He and Kelsey drove out to the HJ early the following morning and found everybody at breakfast.

Hashknife left the table and met them at the porch. Kelsey introduced them, and Cates lost no time in telling Hashknife who he was and why he was in the Tumbling River country.

"But I can't do any good here, Hartley. I was talking with the sheriff about the case, and I told him it was a deal that required a man like you. I hadn't the slightest idea that you were here in the country. Yes, we've heard a lot about you and your ability. I am sure the company will pay you well for your services, and all I have to do is to send a wire."

"But there ain't nothin' to it, except catchin' Joe Rich," said Hashknife. "I don't know this country, Cates. When the sheriff's office, bein' familiar with the country, can't get him, what chance would a stranger have? Anyway, I'm not a manhunter, Cates."

"No?" Cates lifted his eyebrows slightly. "Perhaps some of the stories I've heard were not true."

"They hardly ever are," seriously. "No, you've got me wrong, Cates. Never in my life did I go out and get a man who was wanted by the law—never took a man with a price on his head. That's a job for a sheriff or a policeman."

"Well, maybe that's true, Hartley. There's a nice reward for Joe Rich. Means about thirty-five hundred dollars."

"I don't want it," said Hashknife flatly.

"Don't want it?" Cates laughed huskily. "You're a queer bird, Hartley. Ain't you interested in putting criminals behind the bars?"

"Not a damned bit. Don't believe in the 'eye for an eye' theory. Never put a man behind the bars that I didn't wish it hadn't happened."

"Do yuh mean to say that you never collected a reward?" asked Kelsey.

"Never."

Kelsey laughed shortly.

"You must be pretty rich to turn down good money. Cates has told me that you and yore pardner have cleaned up a lot of bad-man outfits, and there's usually a reward for a bad man."

"Unless he hides his light under a bushel, Kelsey."

"Uh-huh. Well, Joe Rich don't hide his, that's a cinch."

Hashknife grinned widely.

"You've got to admire him, just the same. He's operatin' in his own country, and he ain't tryin' to disguise himself a whole lot. And it looks to me as though he's makin' a monkey out of yore office."

"What do yuh mean, Hartley?"

"By stayin' around here. It don't look to me as though he was scared of yuh, Kelsey."

"I see what yuh mean."

"Well, can't I induce you to work with us, Hartley?" asked Cates. "I can put you on the pay-roll in thirty minutes after I get back to town. I tell you, I'm helpless; and the sheriff admits that he can't do anything."

Hashknife shook his head slowly.

"No-o-o, I'm not interested, Cates. As I said before it's just a case of goin' out and gettin' a man who knows every blade of grass in this country by its first name. What the sheriff ought to do is to make up a posse and comb this whole country. He must be hidin' in the valley."

"Fine chance!" snorted Kelsey. "In the first place I'd have a hard time gettin' any men. Joe is too popular. And in the second place, with all the friends Joe's got—well, figure it out for yourself."

"Do yuh think somebody is hidin' him, Kelsey?"

"I won't say that, but it could happen."

"Yeah, I think so," nodded Hashknife.

"Well, then you don't care to come in on the deal, eh?" queried Cates.

"Nope. Oh, I'm much obliged to yuh and all that, but it's out of my line, Cates. I wish yuh luck."

Cates laughed sourly.

"I'll need it, Hartley."

They shook hands with Hashknife and went back to their buggy. Hashknife watched them ride away and turned to see Sleepy and Honey standing in the doorway.

"We snuck out and listened," said Honey truthfully.

Hashknife smiled at them and rolled a cigarette.

"It kinda looks to me as though the law is stuck," observed Honey.

"It is," smiled Hashknife.

He scratched a match on the steps, lighted his cigarette and turned to Honey.

"Honey, who is there in this country that likes Joe Rich and didn't like Jim Wheeler?"

Honey scratched his elbow on his hip and blinked.

"Never heard of anythin' like that," he said. "Everybody liked Jim, and everybody liked Joe. What'sa idea, Hashknife?"

"Just curiosity. Everybody knows that Joe Rich stole that five thousand from Jim Wheeler, and the sheriff thinks somebody is hidin' Joe."

"I see yore idea. He thinks Joe is bein' taken care of by somebody, eh?"

"That's the only solution, Honey. He's got to eat and have a place to hide out. It must be somebody that likes Joe too well to turn him in for the reward—somebody that don't care about the loss of the HJ."

"By golly, that's right! But who could it be?"

"That's it," grumbled Sleepy.

"Well, he could 'a' made out long enough to have robbed the train," said Honey. "He's prob'ly high-tailin' it out of the country right now. It looks to me as though he's about twenty-five thousand dollars ahead of the game, and a man's a fool who never knows when he's got enough."

"Easy money," said Hashknife thoughtfully. "No man ever quits takin' easy money."

"Yuh don't think he'll try it again, do yuh?" asked Honey.

"From my point of view—yeah, I think he will, Honey."

Honey snorted and threw away his cigarette.

"I'll betcha he's pullin' away from here awful fast. Joe ain't no fool. I'll bet he knows when he's had enough."

"Might be," said Hashknife. "But I doubt it. Suppose we ride over to town and have a look around."

Sleepy and Honey were more than willing. They told the girls they would be back for supper. Peggy drew Hashknife aside and wanted to know what the sheriff had in mind. Hashknife told her frankly that Cates was a detective, and wanted him to help find Joe Rich.

"Just why did he want you to help?" she asked.

"Well, yuh see, it's like this," lied Hashknife. "Kelsey's got the idea that folks around here are too friendly with Joe to hunt him. Me and Sleepy, bein' strangers to Joe, might not be so particular."

"Oh, I see. And are you going to help him?"

"No-o-o-o—I'm goin' to help us find him, Peggy."

"But what good will that do?"

"Any 'good' is better than we've got, Peggy."

"I suppose it is," she sighed. "But I can't see where it will help anybody. If the law gets him—"

"Mebbe—and mebbe not."

"What do you mean, Hashknife?"

"I was just thinkin' out loud, Peggy. Yuh quit worrying about things." He patted her on the arm. "We'll be back for supper, and I'll want to see yuh grinnin'."

Hashknife went out to his horse, which was the one Jim Wheeler had ridden the day he was killed. Hashknife noticed that the animal was a trifle sore-footed; so he examined its hoofs and found that it wore no shoes.

He pulled the saddle off and put it on a chunky bay, turning the sore-footed one back in the corral. The bay was shod in front.

"Jim said somethin' about goin' to have that bronc shod," said Honey. "I remember him speakin' about it a week before he was killed."

"I hate to see a horse limp," said Hashknife. "I'd a lot rather walk."

They rode to Pinnacle City and Hashknife left Sleepy and Honey at the Pinnacle Saloon, where several more cowboys were arguing at the bar. After inquiring at the store, Hashknife found old Doctor Curzon's office.

The old doctor was not busy. He considered Hashknife gravely when Hashknife asked him about the death of Jim Wheeler.

"Well, just what did you wish to know?" he asked.

"All about it," smiled Hashknife. "They tell me Jim Wheeler died from concussion of the brain."

"You might call it that. His skull was crushed. Wonder he lived at all."

"And they tell me that his skull was crushed by the rocks."

"No doubt of it. I don't believe you told me your name."

"Hartley. I'm out at the HJ ranch—Jim Wheeler's place."

"Oh, yes. No, I don't think there is any doubt of Wheeler's head having been crushed by the rocks. You know how a body would bound, fastened by one foot to a stirrup."

"The rocks cut kinda deep, didn't they, Doc?"

"Mm-m-m-m—well, yes."

"Do yuh know—it's a funny thing, Doc?"

"What is?"

"The fact that there ain't a rock as big as a pea on that whole stretch of road where Wheeler was dragged."

"You say there isn't?"

"Well," smiled Hashknife, "I said 'there ain't.' It amounts to the same thing, I suppose. Your English is better than mine."

"But there must be rocks along there," insisted the doctor. "Every one seemed to take it for granted that—"

"That's the trouble, Doc—takin' it for granted. I looked it over the day after the rain, when the dust was settled; and it's as smooth as a billiard-table; not even a humpy spot on the road or along it. Go out and see for yourself."

"Well, well! No, I'll take your word for it. You don't look like a person who would lie about it. You have very good eyes, my friend."

"Thanks," smiled Hashknife.

"But to get back to Jim Wheeler. I believe it was Joe Rich who discovered him first after the accident. They tell queer tales about Joe Rich. I knew him."

"Like him?"

"Very much. He—I believe he said that the foot was still in the stirrup."

"This wound on the head," said Hashknife. "Just where was it the worst, Doc?"

"Nearly on the crown. In fact it extended from just above the left ear to the top of the head. Of course, it is easily possible for the horse to have struck him with a sharp-shod hoof."

"On top of the head, Doc?"

"Well, barely possible. Come to think of it, the wound did have that appearance; as though a horseshoe might have crushed the skull."

"His horse wasn't shod, Doc."

"It wasn't shod?"

The old doctor ran his hand through his white hair and squinted gravely.

"Hadn't been for weeks," said Hashknife.

"You are a detective?" asked the doctor quickly.

Hashknife smiled and shook his head.

"No, Doc; just curious."

"Mm-m-m-m-m," the doctor studied the ceiling of his office. "No rocks, no shoes. But the man had been dragged, Hartley. The skin showed evidence of that, and his shirt was rubbed through. More than that, his leg had been broken from a twist, and the pull of the stirrup."

"Look at it this way," suggested Hashknife. "Suppose Jim Wheeler met a man, who stopped him. This man strikes Wheeler over the head with a gun, knocking him off the saddle. Then this man robs him. Perhaps this man hooked one of Wheeler's feet in the stirrup, struck the horse and let it run away. Or, again, the foot might have hung in the stirrup when the man fell from the horse. Wouldn't it look as though it had been an accident?"

"No doubt of it, my friend. And in that case, it would appear that Joe Rich had not only robbed Jim Wheeler, but had murdered him as well."

"There's a lot of ways to look at it, Doc," smiled Hashknife, as he shook hands with the doctor. "I'm sure much obliged to yuh for yore help in this matter. Yuh would be doin' me another favour, if yuh don't tell anybody what we talked about."

"The ethics of my profession preclude such a thing."

"Well, thanks just the same, Doc. So-long."

Hashknife went back to the Pinnacle, where he found Honey and Sleepy buying drinks for the Heavenly Triplets, the three boys from the Flying H. They tried to get Hashknife to join them, but he was in no mood to join their festivities. After telling Sleepy he was going back to the ranch, he mounted and rode out of town.

Hashknife was satisfied after his talk with the doctor, that Jim Wheeler had not died through an accident. That Joe Rich should have found Wheeler dragged to unconsciousness and have robbed him was too much for Hashknife to believe. Rich had been knocked down by Wheeler and Hashknife, not knowing Rich, would not have any idea of Rich's nature.

As Hashknife neared the spot where Wheeler had been found he saw two saddled horses standing near the road. He drew rein and rode slowly along, wondering where the riders might be. Then he saw them about fifty feet off the road, looking around in some weeds and low brush.

They were Len Kelsey and Jack Ralston. They did not see Hashknife until he was almost up to their horses. Then they left off their search and came over to him.

"Howdy, gents," grinned Hashknife.

Kelsey showed a slight embarrassment but nodded pleasantly.

"Just lookin' around," he said, as if his actions demanded an explanation. "This is where they found Jim Wheeler, yuh know."

"That's what they tell me. I reckon the rain wiped out any tracks yuh might expect to find."

"Yeah, it did," said Ralston quickly. "We found that out."

"No sign of Joe Rich, eh?"

"Not a single sign!" snapped Kelsey, swinging into his saddle.

"I reckon he's a pretty smart lad," said Hashknife. "What became of the detective?"

"He's in town," said Kelsey. "You should have taken him up on that deal, Hartley. Made good wages out of it, even if yuh couldn't find Joe Rich."

"No-o-o-o, I didn't want the job. Joe's got too many good friends around here, Kelsey; and I might stop a bullet, if I knew too much."

"There's a lot of truth in that, Hartley."

"Sure," grinned Hashknife. "I'm no fool."

"Playin' safe, eh?" said Ralston. "Well, I don't blame yuh. When a feller's a stranger, he can't be too careful."

"I'll watch my own hide," declared Hashknife. "I dunno where that feller, Cates, heard all that stuff about me. He must 'a' got me mixed with somebody else. Anyway, he's all wrong if he thinks I'm huntin' rewards."

"Well," laughed Kelsey, "he told me he didn't believe half he had heard about yuh."

"I'm shore glad about that," said Hashknife simply. "Well, I've got to be movin' along gents. Good huntin' to yuh."

Hashknife rode on toward the ranch, while Kelsey and his deputy went on to Pinnacle City. Kelsey swore softly at sight of the Heavenly Triplets' horses at the Pinnacle rack.

"There's two HJ broncs there too," observed Ralston. "That means Honey Bee and Stevens. I don't reckon we'll have much to do with the Pinnacle as long as they're holdin' forth."

And they were surely holding forth. Sleepy and Honey still had a little money, and the boys from the Flying H were spending their next month's wages. William H. Cates, the detective, had fallen into their toils and was enjoying it.

Also, Mr. Cates was marvelling at the amount of raw liquor they could consume without showing it. Mr. Cates was rather proud of his own ability, but he was beginning to have a hunch that before long he was going to see a lot more men than were actually in the room.

"Thish is lots of fun," he announced.

"Par'ner, you ain't started," declared Lonnie. "You stay with us and we'll show yuh bush'ls 'f di'monds. Oh, yessir, you'll shee lots of'm. We'll show yuh levity, y'betcha."

Supper time came, but none of them was hungry. Darkness came down upon Pinnacle City, and still those six men leaned on the bar, their toasts becoming more and more elaborate. Then Lonnie leaned his forehead against the bar and wept bitterly.

"Thish is all there ish," he announced. "Nothin' t' do. Spen' all day gettin' drunk, and there's nothin' t' do but go home."

"O-o-o-oh, my!" wailed Nebrasky. "Tha's a fac'. The jigger that wrote 'Home Sweet Home' must 'a' never got out. Wha's to be done, I'd crave to get an answer? No entertainment? Can't you think of anythin', Misser Detective?"

Not so Cates. He clung to the bar with both hands.

"Let's all go out to the ranch," suggested Nebrasky.

"Wha' for?" queried Honey. "Uncle Hozie'd hop our necks."

"Le's go for ride," choked Cates. "Need—uk—air."

"That," said Sleepy owlishly, "is a shuggestion."

"I know!" exploded Lonnie. "C'mere."

They followed him outside, much to the relief of the bartender, and Lonnie unfolded his scheme. There were many drawbacks, but each and every one was overcome.

With great difficulty Lonnie Myers and Dan Leach secured their horses at the hitch-rack, and they all weaved their erratic way down to the Pinnacle livery-stable, where they circled to the rear. A shed with a long sloping roof had been added to the stable at some remote time, and within this stable was the hearse.

The door was merely fastened with a hasp. They rolled the old hearse out into the yard and tied two lariat ropes to the end of the tongue. The ancient equipage of the dead was resplendent in a fresh coat of varnish and the four horsetail plumes waved boldly from the corners of the top.

They put Cates inside, because he was unable to climb to the top, while Honey Bee, Sleepy and Nebrasky crowded together on the narrow seat. It was quite a task to get both horses pulling at the same time, but once they got the old hearse rolling it was no trick to keep it rolling.

Around they went into the main street, gaining momentum each moment; so much momentum, in fact, that the horses took notice of things and seemed to desire more distance between themselves and this creaking equipage with the yelping cowboys and flowing plumes.

Lonnie's mount was travelling one side of the street, while Dan's mount seemed to prefer the opposite sidewalk, while the hearse took a fairly straight route up the middle of the street, until almost opposite the Pinnacle City bank. Then Lonnie's horse got tangled up in a hitch-rack and Dan's whirled and started the opposite direction.

Crash! The front wheels of the hearse jack-knifed and struck the sidewalk.

Crash! The end of the swinging tongue took out one of the front windows of the bank, while the hearse lurched to a stand-still with the front wheels against the front of the bank building.

Sleepy was thrown off the seat when the wheels struck the sidewalk and he landed on his hands and knees in the street. The sound of the wreck was audible for quite a distance, and in a few minutes the hearse was surrounded by a curious crowd. There was hardly enough light to see what had happened.

Sleepy staggered across the street and sat down on the sidewalk, feeling very foolish over the whole thing. A horseman rode past him and stopped at the hitch-rack. It was Lonnie Myers. Sleepy went over to him.

"That durned thing headed into the bank," he told Lonnie.

"My God! It did? Whatcha know about that? Where's the rest of the gang?"

"Let's go over and have a look."

No one in the crowd seemed to know who had done it. Kelsey was there, as was Jack Ralston.

"Somebody got pretty smart, it seems to me," growled Kelsey.

"Hey, Kelsey!" yelled a voice, "there's a body inside the hearse."

"My God, it's Cates!" whispered Lonnie. "Let's get away from here before we all get arrested."

They hurried back to the Pinnacle bar where they found Dan Leach and Nebrasky. Nebrasky had a lot of skin off his long nose and Dan limped in one leg. None of them mentioned what had just taken place. They had a drink, after which Lonnie leaned on the bar and wondered where Honey might be.

"The last time I seen him he was goin' toward the bank," said Sleepy dryly. "Prob'ly wanted to borrow some money."

Jack Ralston came in and looked the boys over, but did not say anything. Perhaps he had a fair idea as to who had taken the hearse, but he had no evidence. Apparently these boys were merely having a friendly drink.

"Have any of you gents seen that feller Cates?" he asked.

"Cates?" Lonnie screwed up his eyes. "Oh, yeah—the detective! Why, I think he died, didn't he?" Lonnie turned to Nebrasky.

"Oh, yeah—Cates. Believe he did, Lonnie."

"Uh-huh," Lonnie turned to Ralston. "Yeah, he died. Have a drink, Jack?"

"Nope."

Ralston turned on his heel and went out.

"Ha, ha, ha, ha, ha, ha!" laughed Nebrasky. "Wait'll they find him."

"They found him," said Sleepy. "We'll probably have to pay for that busted window."

"But wasn't it worth it?" chuckled Nebrasky. "I never went higher in my life. There goes the hearse."

They walked to the door and saw several men pulling the hearse back to its shed. They could see a crowd in front of the bank, and apparently there was a man on a ladder, nailing boards over the broken window.

"Where in heck is Honey?" asked Sleepy. "By golly, we're shy one man!"

"That's right. Let's go find him."

They wended their way to the Arapaho saloon, but did not find him there, and then they made a systematic search of every place they could think of.

They finally came past the bank, where they found the object of their search sitting on the sidewalk, holding his head in his hands. Lonnie almost fell over him in the dark.

"Now, where in heck have you been keepin' youself?" demanded Lonnie. "We've been lookin' for yuh for about a week."

This was hardly true, because the accident had not happened more than twenty minutes previous.

Honey lifted his head and wiggled his arms.

"I'm all right, I reckon," he said huskily. "Didn't any of you ord'nary drunks see me go into the bank?"

"See yuh go into the bank?" grunted Nebrasky.

"Abs'lutely! Right through the window! I landed on my chin right in front of the deposit window with one of them horsetail plumes in my right hand."

"And didn't get killed?" wondered Nebrasky.

"Oh, sure, I got killed all right, as far as that's concerned. Oh, my! I heard a lot of folks talkin' about the busted window, while I'm crawlin' around on my hands and knees, trying to find a way out.

"And then I got the scare of my life," Honey laughed foolishly. "I found a man in there."

"Yuh found a man in there?" queried Sleepy quickly.

"Uh-huh. Honest Injun, cross m'heart. He's there yet, too. By golly, it scared me so much that I got right up and walked out the back door. Funniest feelin' yuh—"

"Hold on a minute!" snorted Sleepy. "You walked out the back door, Honey?"

"Shore did, Sleepy."

"Was it unlocked?"

"Must 'a' been—I jist turned the knob. I was on my hands and knees, kinda crawlin' and feelin' along, when I got hold of somethin' that feels a lot like a man's legs. I keeps on feelin', and I keeps on a-risin', until my hands touch his face, and then I high-tailed it outside. I fell down over a box and bumped my head against the building, but kept on goin'. I reckon I plumb circled this side of the street, and just came back here a little while ago."

"Yo're drunk," declared Nebrasky.

"I was drunk," corrected Honey. "But by golly, I was sober a-plenty when I felt that jigger."

"Is he there yet?" asked Lonnie.

"I tell yuh he's roped to the chair!"

"Wait a minute," said Sleepy. "You boys go over to the Pinnacle and let me handle this, will yuh?"

"Go to it," said Lonnie. "C'mon, you fellers."

Sleepy went down the street to the sheriff's office. He was perfectly sober and none the worse for their escapade, except for a slightly skinned knee. Both Kelsey and Ralston were at the office when Sleepy came in.

"Yuh better investigate the bank," said Sleepy. "I just came past there, and I thought I heard a man groanin'."

"Yeah?" Kelsey grinned knowingly. "Yuh did, eh? Just what kind of a game are you punchers tryin' to pull off now?"

"Oh, well, go ahead and be a flaming fool," sighed Sleepy, turning back to the door. "I'm tellin' yuh what I heard, tha'sall."

But Kelsey stopped him at the door.

"Yuh think yuh heard a man groanin', eh?"

"It don't make any difference," said Sleepy. "Go on to bed. I'll find the man that owns the bank, and he'll probably be interested."

"If this is a joke—" warned Kelsey picking up his hat.

"I better go and get Warner, the cashier," said Ralston. "He rooms at MacRae's place."

Ralston trotted down the street while Kelsey followed Sleepy back to the front of the bank. They listened at the broken window, which had been barred with some planks, but could hear nothing.

"Yuh probably heard the wind blowing," said Kelsey.

"What wind?" asked Sleepy.

Kelsey didn't explain just which wind he had meant, as there was not a breath of air stirring. In a few minutes Ralston joined them, panting from his run.

"Warner ain't been there since supper, Len. He was workin' tonight, they said."

"And Old Man Ludlow, the president, is on a trip to the coast," said Len. "How in hell are we goin' to find out anythin'?"

"Smash out another window," suggested Ralston.

"How about the back door?" asked Sleepy.

They went around to the back and found the door sagging open. Kelsey swore softly and led the way inside, where they lighted matches to guide them. And they found just what Honey Bee had found—a man roped to a chair and gagged. It was Warner, the cashier, his eyes blinking foolishly at the light of Kelsey's match, whilst Ralston took a pocket-knife and severed the lariat rope which bound him.

Warner was apparently unhurt. After they untied the gag he worked his jaw painfully, rubbed his lips and managed to get back a measure of his speech.

Sleepy found a lamp, which he lighted, and the three men watched the cashier stretch his arms and legs, grimacing as the returning circulation pained him.

"You better send a wire to Old Man Ludlow," he said huskily. "Palace Hotel, San Francisco. The bank has been cleaned out."

"Cleaned out, Warner?" asked Kelsey.

"Look at the vault door."

It was wide open. The sheriff did not investigate. Sleepy stepped over and peered inside. It was an old-fashioned vault with the ordinary combination. Time locks had not come to Pinnacle City yet.

"How many in the gang?" asked Kelsey.

"One," Warner spat painfully and rubbed his lips. "One man, Sheriff. I was working tonight. I used the back door. When I unlocked it and stepped outside, this man confronted me with a gun and forced me back inside.

"I refused to open the vault—at first. But he produced some dynamite and told me he was going to blow it open. He said he would tie me close enough to see it bust. There wasn't anything for me to do except to open it. Then he roped me to a chair, put a gag in my mouth and helped himself. There was enough light through that side window for me to see that he put everything in a sack."

"Masked?" asked Kelsey.

"Yes. I wish one of you would wire Ludlow. What was that crash that broke the front window?"

"Some drunken cowboys," growled Kelsey. "How long before that did the robbery take place?"

"Possibly fifteen minutes. Might have been longer. But there was another man in here after that crash. I couldn't see what he looked like, but he felt all over me, and then I heard him go out through the back door."

Kelsey squinted closely at Sleepy, but Sleepy looked very innocent. His blue eyes did not waver for an instant.

"Pretty queer!" snorted Kelsey.

"Ain't it?" agreed Sleepy. "Queerest thing I ever heard."

"It might have been the man who tied me up," said Warner.

Warner was a small, thin-faced man, slightly stooped, wearing steel-bowed glasses. He took them from his pocket and hooked the bows over his ears, his hands trembling.

"Might have been," agreed Sleepy. "Prob'ly took him quite a while to clean out the place. How much did he get?"

"I can't tell you that, sir. I think Mr. Ludlow would like to hear about it as soon as possible."

"No hurry; he can't help any," said Kelsey. "Warner, did you get a good look at this robber?"

"It was dark in here. He held a match in his left hand while I worked the combination."

"Did, eh?" Kelsey seemed interested. "Well, how much of him didja see, Warner?"

"Not much, I'm afraid; only that arm in the light. You see, he stood rather behind me."

"All right; and didja see that arm well enough to tell what it looked like?"

"Yes, I saw it well enough, I think. It—it looked like a—a—well, just like an arm," he finished weakly.

"That's fine," sneered Kelsey. "All we've got to do is to find a man who has a left arm that looks like an arm. Didn't yuh see his clothes, his hands, his gun?"

"Yes, I—I saw his gun. Certainly I saw his gun."

"Was it like this one?" Kelsey jerked out his Colt and held it in front of Warner.

"No, not exactly. I think it had a white handle."

"Ah-hah! Now, about his sleeve, Warner. Did he wear leather cuffs?"

"Yes, yes! I forgot them. Black, I think. Perhaps they merely looked black. But the matchlight—there were silver ornaments, Sheriff. I remember now—silver stars. It's funny I didn't remember before."

"Uh-huh. We'll go and send that wire to Ludlow, Warner. Lock that back door, will yuh, Warner. Not much use, at that; nothin' left to steal. Mebbe yuh better shut that vault door and spin the combination."

Warner went with the sheriff and deputy, while Sleepy cut across the street and found the rest of the boys in front of the Pinnacle. From there they could see the light in the bank, and they were burning with curiosity.

"Forget what you know, Honey," warned Sleepy. "The rest of yuh don't know a thing; *sabe*? The bank was cleaned out by a lone bandit fifteen minutes ahead of our smash. The man Honey found was Warner, the cashier. He was roped and gagged, but he wasn't knocked out."

"Ye don't say?" snorted Honey. "That was it, eh?"

"Yeah, and we better all head for home," advised Sleepy. "We don't know a thing. The bank is as clean as a hound's tooth and the man who cleaned it out wore silver stars on his cuffs and used a white-handled gun. Let's mosey."

They all got their horses and headed out of town, the Heavenly Triplets going to the Flying H, while Honey and Sleepy rode swiftly out to the HJ where they woke Hashknife in the bunk-house and told him their story. He sat up in bed and smoked a cigarette, his lean fingers scratching at his unruly hair.

"It looks to me as though Joe Rich missed his callin' when he got himself elected sheriff," he said slowly. "That boy shore is featherin' his nest. And yuh had Mr. Cates laid out in the hearse, eh?"

"Fit to be buried," nodded Sleepy. "I reckon he was the only one that didn't do a high dive. That little cashier shore was scared. The robber told him he'd either open the safe or get a front seat at the explosion. And he held a match while the cashier worked the combination. By golly, it's so easy to do a thing like that, that I wonder why men work for a dollar a day! It's shore easy money."

"Easy to get, uneasy to keep, Sleepy."

"Yea-a-a-ah! Who, I ask ye, is goin' to get it away from him? You can preach honesty to me all yuh want to, cowboy, but when I see a job done as easy as that one—"

"Aw, c'mon to bed, and stop yappin'. I want to think."

CHAPTER VIII:
CLUES

Nothing had ever happened in Pinnacle City that caused as much excitement as the robbery of the bank. It was something that affected nearly everybody in the Tumbling River country. As Uncle Hozie expressed it—

"There's a lot of flat pocketbooks right now."

The news spread swiftly, and by noon of the following day the town was filled with range-folk. The sheriff came in for the usual amount of criticism, and a number of the cattlemen sat in his office, trying to help him devise ways and means of putting a stop to Joe Rich's activities. A wire had been received from Old Man Ludlow, the president of the bank, who was on his way back to Pinnacle.

Uncle Hozie mourned the loss of eight thousand dollars, while Ed Merrick swore himself red in the face over half that amount. He had drawn out five thousand to lend to Jim Wheeler, thus cutting down his bank deposit.

But they were all losers; some of them more so than others, and Joe Rich's latest robbery bid fair to make times rather hard in Tumbling River. It was a privately owned bank, and they knew that Ludlow could not make good their losses.

William H. Cates took the first train out of town. The sheriff had hauled him out of the hearse and put him to bed. The following morning he was filled with remorse over it all, but strangely enough he was unable to tell just whom he had been with. He told the sheriff to do his little best and boarded a train for the north.

An examination of the vault disclosed the fact that the robber had taken every cent of money, but had not bothered with any papers. Warner refused even to make a guess at how much money was in the vault, but admitted that it was more than was usually carried. The bank remained closed.

Hashknife, Sleepy and Honey came back to town that forenoon, but the Heavenly Triplets did not show up. Merrick talked with Hashknife about the robbery. Hashknife was not interested to any great extent.

A little later on Hashknife was talking with Kelsey, when the depot agent came to Kelsey.

"Here's a funny thing," said the agent. "Remember the night the bridge caught fire?"

"Sure," nodded Kelsey. "What about it?"

"That night," resumed the agent, "the rear brakeman of the cattle-train went back to flag the passenger, and he's never been seen since."

"What do yuh mean?" Kelsey was evidently puzzled.

"Just what I said. I don't know how he was passed up. The train was held here quite a while, but the storm was bad, and nobody needed him, I suppose. Down at the bridge both trains were stalled quite a while, and there was no need of whistling in the flag from the cattle-train.

"Oh, the company missed him the next day. But he was what is known as a boomer brakeman, and they just thought he had stepped out without drawing his pay. They do that once in a while—those boomers. But later on they got to checking up on things, and the conductor remembered that he hadn't seen this man since the night at the bridge. Ransome is the division point, you see; so he didn't have much farther to go. The reason they watered that stock here was because there were better facilities than at Ransome."

"Well, that's kinda queer," said Kelsey.

"I saw him go out to flag," said Hashknife. "I remember that freight conductor blamed the passenger crew for runnin' past the flag. They said they never seen it."

"Well, what do you suppose happened to him?" queried Kelsey.

"Search me," said the depot agent. "All I know is what I heard over the wire."

Hashknife left the sheriff and found Sleepy and Honey. He told them what the depot agent had said. A few minutes later they were heading for the railroad bridge, going through the country where Hashknife and Sleepy had walked the night of the bridge-fire. They tied their horses to the right-of-way fence, crawled through and climbed up to the track level.

The railroad had been graded along the side of the hill, so that the opposite side dropped off about twenty or thirty feet, where the brush grew thick along the fence. Hashknife estimated where the rear end of the cattle-train would have been, and they walked back along the track to the first curve.

Just beyond that there was considerable seepage of water on the lower side, where grew a profusion of tules and cat-tails, mingled with wild-roses and willows. The bank was rather abrupt along here and heavy brush grew between the track and the upper fence.

Hashknife slid cautiously down this bank, hooking his heels into the broken rock. There was more water, covered with a greenish slime.

"Hook yore heels, cowboy," laughed Sleepy. "One little mistake, and you take a green-water bath."

Hashknife worked down to the water edge and went slowly along about fifty feet. Then he stopped and sat back against the bank. For several moments he studied the tangle of brush and green water. Then he turned his head and looked up at the two men above him.

"I've found him," he said.

"You've found him?" gasped Honey.

"Uh-huh. One foot still on dry land. I thought it was just an old shoe. He must 'a' went in head first. There's his lantern in the muck—just the bottom of it stickin' out."

Hashknife turned around and climbed up the bank. From the track level he could not see the shoe nor the lantern. He heaped up a pile of stones beside the track to mark the spot.

"Ain't we goin' to take him out?" asked Sleepy.

"Not me," replied Hashknife. "That's the sheriff's job."

They rode back to the ranch and were just debating what to do, when Ben Collins came along on his way to town from the Circle M. Honey called to him and he stopped at the HJ gate.

"You'll probably see Kelsey in town," said Honey. "Tell him we found the brakeman of that cattle-train. He's in the ditch on the west side of the railroad track, about three hundred yards south of the bridge. We heaped up a pile of rocks along the track, and the body is straight down from that. Tell Kelsey he'll need help to get the body."

Collins stared at Honey, his mouth agape. It was all Greek to him, it seemed.

"Well, I'll be bust!" he snorted. "Let me get this straight."

He repeated what Honey had told him, making a few mistakes, which Honey rectified.

"But who killed him?" he demanded.

"We don't know, Ben."

"Well, I'll be damned! All right, I'll tell him."

Ben spurred his horse to a gallop and was soon out of sight.

"They'll have to come through this way to get him, won't they?" asked Hashknife.

"Unless they want to carry the body across the railroad bridge. Good gosh, things look worse for Joe Rich every day! I suppose he ran into the brakeman, eh?"

"Probably," nodded Hashknife. "Of course he might have fell off the track that night. The wind was awful. If he struck his head on the rocks and slid into the water he'd die pretty quick. We'll have to wait until they take him out."

But they didn't have to wait long. Inside an hour Kelsey, Ralston, Ben Collins and Abe Liston of the 3W3, rode in at the HJ. No one had told Peggy and Laura about the dead man, and their curiosity was aroused by the advent of the sheriff and his men.

"Man got hit by a train out by the bridge," said Hashknife.

"Was he killed?" asked Laura.

"I reckon he was."

Hashknife went out and talked with Kelsey, who seemed a trifle sore about their finding the body.

"I suppose yuh fooled around and wiped out all the clues," he said complainingly.

"Well, I dunno," smiled Hashknife. "We didn't go near the body, Sheriff."

"Didn't, eh? Seems to me you was in a bit of a sweat to get out there ahead of the law."

"Did look thataway." Hashknife did not cease smiling with his mouth, although his eyes were serious.

"Just how do yuh figure this yore affair, Hartley?"

"You do the figurin'," suggested Hashknife.

The sheriff glanced keenly at Hashknife's eyes and decided to drop the subject.

"Oh, all right," he said. "Yuh might come along and help us take the body out."

"Yeah, I might," said Hashknife. "But I don't think I will. You've got plenty men with yuh."

"Uh-huh." Kelsey did not press the invitation, but rode away, followed by his three men.

Honey Bee grinned widely and did a shuffle in the dirt.

"That's tellin' 'em, cowboy. You've got Kelsey's goat. I could see it in his face."

"Let's go down to the bunk-house," suggested Hashknife. "Them darned girls ask too many questions. I reckon they suspect that this man was killed at that hold-up, and I don't want to worry Peggy any more. She takes it too serious. By golly, she acts as though folks blamed her for what Joe Rich has done."

"That's Peggy," sighed Honey. "Whitest little girl that ever lived. Suppose we have a three-handed game of seven-up for a million dollars a corner."

"You two go ahead," said Hashknife. "I've got to think a while."

"Don't yore head ever hurt yuh?" asked Honey. "You've done an awful lot of thinkin' since I knew yuh, Hashknife."

"He has to think an awful lot to get a little ways," grinned Sleepy.

Sleepy and Honey went into the bunk-house, and Laura wig-wagged to Hashknife from the veranda of the ranch-house.

"What about this dead man?" she demanded.

"Dunno yet, Laura. He's dead, but we don't know what killed him."

He told her about the missing brakeman. Laura had been doing a little thinking, and she confided to Hashknife that she was afraid that Jim Wheeler had been killed by the man who stole the money.

"Aunt Emma thinks so too," she said. "We had a talk about it the other day. Joe was out here that day, you know. He came to tell Peggy good-bye. His lips were cut badly and he looked awful bad. But Peggy didn't tell him good-bye. She was crying and didn't hear him go away. She thought he was still there. We found out later that Uncle Jim had knocked Joe down on the street in Pinnacle City."

Hashknife nodded over this. He had heard it before.

"But she still loves Joe Rich."

"I honestly think she does," agreed Laura.

"Did yuh hear about them findin' Joe's pocket-knife in the express car?"

Laura hadn't heard about it.

"The knife that Peggy gave him for his birthday? Oh, what an awful thing to do! Criminals always make mistakes, don't they?"

"Yeah, they shore do, Laura—bad ones, too."

Peggy came out on the veranda and sat down with them.

"Tell me about that bank robbery," she said to Hashknife.

The tall cowboy sighed and reshaped the crown of his hat.

"There ain't much to tell, Peggy. A lone man met the cashier at the rear door of the bank, forced him back, made him open the vault and then roped and gagged the cashier. They say he got away with a lot of money. Wasn't anybody hurt."

"What was the description of that man, Hashknife?"

"Wasn't any—much. Yuh see, it was dark in there."

"Much?" sighed Peggy. "Oh, I know!" she suddenly blurted. "You try to cover it. Please don't do that, Hashknife."

Hashknife shook his head sadly.

"That cashier was probably scared stiff, Peggy. Power of suggestion made him see what the express messenger saw—the black leather cuffs with the silver stars. Discount all that stuff. Keep smilin', I tell yuh. A-a-aw, shucks!"

Hashknife jumped to his feet and walked away. Peggy was crying, and Hashknife couldn't stand tears. He went down and sat against the stable, his hat pulled down over his eyes. And he was still there when the sheriff and his men came back, bringing the body of the brakeman, strapped across the saddle of Jack Ralston's horse, while Jack rode behind Kelsey. The body was covered with a dirty tarpaulin.

Hashknife went out to meet them, and Kelsey thanked him for the marker.

"It shore was well hidden," he said, "and them rocks helped a lot. I reckon this will kinda swell the reward for Joe Rich, Hartley. This man was shot. Yuh can even see the powder marks on his coat, so it must 'a' been close work. We'll shore ask for Joe Rich dead or alive now."

They rode on, and Hashknife leaned against the stable, his mind working swiftly. Dead or alive!

"Oh, I was afraid of that," he told himself.

He saddled his horse and went to the bunk-house, where he called to the boys.

"I'm goin' to town," he told them. "They just went past with that body. The man was shot at close range, and they'll offer a reward for Joe Rich, dead or alive. I want to get a look at that body. Be back for supper, and for gosh sake, don't let Peggy know what they said!"

Hashknife galloped away from the ranch, but did not try to overtake the sheriff and his party. They took the body straight to the doctor's office. It happened that Doctor Curzon was the county coroner, and the case would require an inquest.

But the sheriff and his party did not stay more than fifteen minutes; so Hashknife waited until they were out of sight before he rode up to the doctor's little home.

The old doctor greeted him gravely and started to tell him about the latest tragedy, but Hashknife stopped him.

"I know all about it, Doc. What about that bullet? Did it go all the way through?"

The doctor nodded.

"Yes, it did."

Hashknife sighed. He had hopes that the calibre of the bullet might give him a clue. The doctor showed him the body. There was no mistaking the corpse. It was that of the brakeman, but little changed from immersion. The bullet had gone straight through his heart, and he had probably plunged straight off the high bank into the slough.

"Poor devil," sighed Hashknife. "Anyway, he died quick, Doc. The wind was blowin' away from us, so we had no chance to hear the sound of the shot. Anyway, I'm much obliged."

"You're certainly welcome, sir. We will probably hold an inquest tomorrow, and perhaps the sheriff will ask you to attend as a witness."

"All right, Doc."

Hashknife led his horse up to the main street and over to the Pinnacle hitch-rack. Just beyond the hitch-rack was the end of the board sidewalk which led down past the saloon. This end of the sidewalk was about two feet higher than the ground level. It had been intended to continue the walk, but this had never been done. Pedestrians usually ignored the sidewalk at this point and went farther along, where the contour of the ground permitted a lower step.

Hashknife sat down on the end of this sidewalk, bracing his shoulders against the corner of the building, and rolled a smoke. The sheriff was at his office, talking with the depot agent, who was writing a telegram to send to the railroad company at Ransome.

Ben Collins' and Abe Liston's horses were at the Pinnacle hitch-rack; so Hashknife surmised that they were retailing the story in the saloon. Two youngsters came from the rear of the building, barefooted, overalls-clad. One of them had a ball made of rags sewed through with heavy thread; rather a lop-sided affair, but a ball, for all that.

Hashknife smiled at them and they grinned back at him.

"Throw me a catch," he said, holding out his hands.

The boy with the ball flipped it toward Hashknife, but his aim was faulty and the ball struck the ground several feet in front of Hashknife. It failed to bounce, but rolled heavily under the sidewalk.

"Bum throwin'!" shrilled the other youngster.

Hashknife laughed and dropped to his knees, crawling beneath the sidewalk trying to reach the ball.

"Lemme help yuh, mister," said the boy who owned the ball.

"I can get it," said Hashknife.

He picked it up and handed it absently back to the boy. In the accumulated litter of old playing cards, miscellaneous pieces of paper and the general débris, his eyes caught sight of a certain piece of paper.

"Can'tcha git out?" asked the boy who had the ball.

Hashknife backed out. He had forgotten the boys. In his hand was a folded piece of paper, which he unfolded and read carefully. It was Jim Wheeler's copy of the note on which he had borrowed the money from Ed Merrick.

"Now, how in hell did that get under there?" wondered Hashknife. He studied the situation. Close to this spot was the hitch-rack.

"He got on his horse at that rack," said Hashknife to himself. "He thought he put the note in his pocket, but didn't; and the wind blew it under the sidewalk. No wonder he didn't have the note when they found him."

He folded the note and put it carefully in his pocket. The two youngsters were watching him closely, possibly wondering what he had found. Hashknife stared at them for a moment, and a grin came to his lips as he dug down in his pocket and drew out two quarters.

"You boys buy yoreselves some candy," he said giving them the money.

"Thank yuh, mister!" exploded one of them, and they raced across the street to a store, all out of breath. Hashknife went to his horse, mounted and rode out of town.

The two boys lined up at the fly-specked candy counter and took plenty of time in picking out what they wanted. Angus McLaren and Len Kelsey came into the store, talking earnestly about the latest developments, and stopped near the two boys.

The old man behind the counter peered over his glasses at the boys.

"Yuh want two-bits' worth apiece?" he asked, rather awed at their enormous purchases. "By golly, yuh must have struck a soap mine!"

"Didn't strike no mine," said one of them. "How much are them chaklits, Mr. Becker?"

"Aw, you don't want no chaklits!" snorted the other. "They don't give yuh hardly any for a dime. Gimme some mixed."

"I want some mixed, too, Mr. Becker, but I don't want all of it mixed."

One of the boys turned and saw the sheriff and McLaren, who were smiling at them.

"Got two-bits apiece," grinned the boy. "A tall cowpuncher gave it to us."

"He's that new puncher at the HJ," explained the other.

"Gave yuh each two-bits?" smiled McLaren. "That was generous of him, eh?"

"Y'betcha. Over by the Pinnacle Saloon rack. I threw my ball to him an' it went under the end of the sidewalk. He got under after it, an' he found somethin', I think. Anyway, he was lookin' at a paper when he got out, an' he gave us each two-bits."

"What kind of a piece of paper?" asked McLaren.

"I seen it," said the other boy, watching the merchant weigh the candy. "It was kinda folded up—had printin' on it. Say, Mr. Becker, are yuh sure them scales don't weight under?"

They paid for their candy and went outside, looking into their sacks.

"That must have been Hartley," said Kelsey. "He didn't lose any time in followin' us to town. He was at the HJ when we brought the body past there. I wonder what he found?"

McLaren shook his head. He hadn't any idea nor was he interested in knowing.

Kelsey went back to the court-house, where he found Fred Coburn, the county attorney, at his office. He laid the facts of the case before Coburn, who listened to Kelsey's story of finding the body of the brakeman.

"All right," said Coburn briskly. "Make out a new reward notice, Len. Offer the reward, dead or alive. I'll file a charge of first degree murder against Rich.

Personally I think he killed Jim Wheeler, although that would be hard to make stick. This is a cinch. Better see if the commissioners don't want to boost that reward. When Ludlow comes I'm sure the bank will boost it. Rich is going to make one break too many—and we'll get him."

"That's a cinch, Coburn. See yuh later."

As he came from the attorney's office he met Ed Merrick, Angus McLaren and Ross Layton, the three commissioners.

"I was just going to look for you fellers," he said. "Just had a talk with Coburn about the reward. He's goin' to file first degree murder against Joe Rich and wants me to make up a new reward notice, offering it for him, dead or alive. How about boostin' the ante, eh?"

McLaren shook his head quickly.

"I'm not in favour of it. There's already thirty-five hundred offered, and I've no doubt the railroad company will add to that for the death of the brakeman."

"It would be worth a lot to have him behind the bars," said Merrick seriously.

"Or under the sod," added Layton.

"Let's boost it another thousand," suggested Merrick. "It won't hurt to make it worth while."

McLaren turned to Layton.

"What do ye say, Ross?"

"Oh, it's all right with me," said the little man, hooking his thumbs inside the armholes of his fancy vest. "Seems to me it's like making conversational bets—they're never won or lost. Personally, I'd like to see more action and less interest in what the man's scalp is worth."

"Ye hit it, Ross," laughed McLaren.

"Well," said Kelsey savagely, "in this country you've just about got to buy a man like Joe Rich."

"Ye mean to make it worth while for somebody to forget friendship, Kelsey?"

"That's just what I mean, McLaren!"

"Oh, well, have it yer own way, lad. Friendship is a great thing, and it's harrd to overcome with silver. As much of a law-abidin' citizen as I am, I'd vote to hang the man that would even betray Joe Rich for money."

"You wouldn't stretch friendship to cover a man who was wanted for murder, would yuh, Mac?" asked Kelsey.

"Friendship," said McLaren heavily, "is ver-ry elastic. If it wasn't there's few of us that would have any."

"By gee, that's true!" snorted Layton. "I guess we'll just leave that reward as it is, Mac."

"All right, yo're the doctors," said Kelsey. "I merely wanted to speed things up a little."

Merrick smiled thinly.

"Joe Rich still has friends," he said meaningly.

McLaren's eyes darkened, but he turned and walked away, with the flowery-vested member from Ransome following in his wake, his black coat-tails flapping, looking very much as Honey Bee had said—"a bouquet of flowers wrapped up in crêpe."

Merrick and Ben Collins rode past the HJ a few hours later and stopped to tell Hashknife that Kelsey wanted him and the other two boys at the inquest on the following day.

"Just a matter of form," said Merrick. "You boys found the body, and I think you were the last persons to see him alive; so the coroner will require your testimony."

"Yeah; all right," agreed Hashknife. "What time?"

"About two o'clock in the afternoon."

Merrick's white teeth flashed in a smile beneath his pointed black moustache as he glanced toward the house, where Laura was standing, looking out toward them.

"Rather a pleasant place to stay, Hartley," he said meaningly.

Hashknife did not reply to this, but his gray eyes suddenly seemed to change colour and became very hard. Merrick shifted his gaze and lifted his reins.

"Well, we'll be amblin' on," he said. "See yuh tomorrow."

Neither Merrick nor Collins said anything until they were well out of earshot, when Collins glanced back and said:

"Don't fool with that jigger, Ed. Holee Saints, didja see his eyes? Didja? It went to forty below right then!"

Merrick nodded grimly.

"I guess that detective wasn't far off when he said that Hartley wasn't all smiles."

Hashknife leaned against the gate-post and watched them fade away in the dust. His eyes were normal now—lazy gray eyes which looked out across the hills, but did not see them; and there was a smile on his wide mouth. Laura was calling him from the veranda and he turned slowly to go back.

It was supper time when Honey and Sleepy came back to the HJ and they brought Slim Coleman with them. They had met Slim near the west end of the bridge, and he rode over with them to have some supper before going back to the Lazy B.

Slim was almost the counterpart of Hashknife physically, being rather a high-pocket sort of individual. The girls welcomed Slim, for he was as one of the family—an old-timer in the Tumbling River and a bunkie of Honey Bee's when Honey was at the Lazy B.

"It's shore tough, this here offerin' of a reward, dead or alive, for Joe Rich," said Slim, who did not have a particle of diplomacy in his system.

Peggy gasped and fled from the room, while Honey proceeded to upbraid Slim for making such a foolish remark before Peggy.

"Well, how'd I know?" wailed Slim. "Nobody told me she was still feelin' right toward Joe."

"Didn't I tell yuh not to talk much about it?" demanded Honey angrily. "I told yuh that when we was crossin' the bridge."

"Yeah, I know you did. But I didn't talk much. I only said it was too bad!"

"Well, that's a lot, Slim. Peggy didn't know they wanted Joe for murder."

"Well, she knows it now. I s'pose I might as well be the one to break the news to her."

"Oh, it don't matter so much," said Hashknife. "She'd find it out tomorrow, anyway. We're all to be called on that inquest—me and Sleepy and Honey. It won't amount to anythin'. They'll just bring in a verdict chargin' Joe with the murder."

"I was talkin' to Ross Layton before we left town," said Honey. "Kelsey is gettin' out new reward notices. He wanted the commissioners to vote more money on that reward, but Ross and Angus McLaren were against it."

"Kelsey's got the idea that some of Joe's friends are hidin' him, and that a bigger reward would make 'em trade him in."

Hashknife laughed heartily.

"That's a new one, Honey. I've heard of lots of reasons for offerin' rewards, but that's the first time I ever heard of tryin' to buy off a friendship."

"Well, that was Kelsey's idea. He's shore a bright sheriff. He thinks that an added reward would cause Joe's friends to pop him on the head and bring him in."

"It might, at that," said Hashknife.

Wong Lee called them to supper, but the two girls did not come to the table.

"Slim, you raised the wind with yore remarks," whispered Honey.

"What do yuh mean?"

"Ruined the girls' appetites."

"Pshaw, I'm sorry about that."

They ate silently for several minutes, and then Slim laid down his knife and fork.

"I found somethin' funny today," he said. "I was ridin' down a coulee, kinda southeast of the Lazy B, and I finds a dead horse. Plenty buzzards feedin'. But the funny part of it is this. That horse had been skinned. Yessir, it shore had. I looked it all over and there ain't a sign of skin on it anywhere. And it kinda looked to me as though somebody had pulled the shoes off it, too. Anyway, it never travelled far after the shoes was taken off."

"Somebody needed horse-hide," observed Honey, helping himself to more food.

"Yeah, I s'pose they did," agreed Slim, resuming his meal. "It ain't a common thing for to skin a dead horse. It ain't been dead a heap of a long time. I didn't smell—"

"Hey!" snorted Honey. "What do yuh think this is? We're eatin' a meal, Slim."

"Oh, I beg yore pardon."

"Could yuh find it again?" asked Hashknife grinning.

"Shore. If the wind's blowin' jist—"

"Wait a minute!" snorted Honey. "You let up on that departed critter, or I'll—I'll—"

"All right, Honey."

"About how long had the animal been dead, Slim?" asked Hashknife.

"Well, I'll tell yuh, Hartley. Judgin' from the—"

"Oh!" exploded Honey.

He kicked back his chair and tramped out through the kitchen to the rear of the house, where he sat down on the well-curb and rolled a smoke.

Slim reached across the table, removed an egg from Honey's plate and placed it on his own.

"I can allus git extra food thataway," he grinned. "Honey ain't very strong. Too much 'magination, I'd say."

They finished their supper and went down to the bunk-house. Slim wanted to play pitch. Hashknife declined to be a party to any card arguments; so he stayed out of the game and went back to the ranch-house, where he found Wong Lee serving supper to Peggy and Laura.

No reference was made to Slim's statement about the reward, but it was rather difficult to find any conversation that did not connect with the troubles of Tumbling River. Laura essayed a few pieces of music on the old upright organ, while Peggy curled up in an old rocker, her chin on one hand. Hashknife sprawled on the sofa, his long legs crossed, while the blue smoke curled up from his cigarette.

"Don't you sing, Hashknife?" Laura turned on the stool and looked at Hashknife.

"Yeah, I sing—sometimes."

"Come and sing us a song."

"No-o-o-o, I don't think so, Laura. I'm what you'd call an absent-minded singer. I never sing when I know just what I'm doin'."

"Joe used to sing," said Peggy simply.

"And he had a good voice, too," added Laura.

There was a long period of silence. Finally Hashknife got to his feet and stood there for a long time, deep in thought. The two girls watched him curiously. Suddenly he looked at them, and a smile spread across his face.

"I just got some good news," he said.

"You got some good news?" Laura got up from the stool and stared at him. "How could you get some good news?"

Hashknife laughed softly and sat down again.

"I just got to thinkin'," he said. "Sometimes I get news thataway. Go ahead and play somethin', Laura."

For possibly an hour Laura played snatches of old songs, playing entirely by ear. Hashknife still sprawled on the sofa, his eyes closed. Several times Laura and Peggy exchanged amused glances, thinking he was asleep, but he was far from it. Finally Laura left the organ, and Hashknife opened his eyes.

"Play another one, Laura," he asked.

"Another one?" The little blonde-headed girl laughed. "Why, I've been playing for over an hour, Hashknife."

"Thasso?" He smiled at her. "That shows how much I enjoyed yore music."

"I don't believe you were listening at all."

"Oh, yeah, I was."

The two girls decided to go to bed and left Hashknife to his cigarette-rolling. For another hour he smoked, only moving to throw a cigarette butt into the fireplace and to roll a fresh one. He had turned the lamp down low when the girls left the room and now he blew out the light, yawned heavily and went to the front door.

It was dark outside and the wind was blowing. He could see the dull glow of a light in the bunk-house window as he stepped off the porch. To the left and to the rear of the bunk-house was the main stable, behind which was part of the corral, which extended out from a front corner of the stable.

Hashknife was half-way to the bunk-house when something attracted his attention. It was down near the stable and sounded very much like a smothered cry. The wind was blowing from that direction. He stopped short, peering through the darkness. There was something moving down near the stable.

Hashknife hurried toward the stable, wondering whether it had been a cry or merely the sound of the stable door in the wind. Then he saw the bulk of a moving horse swinging around as if frightened, and he could hear the bang of the stable door swinging in the wind.

But before he could determine just what was going on, the flame of a revolver shot licked out toward him and he heard the bullet strike the ranch-house. Again and again the gun flashed; but Hashknife had dropped flat and was shooting back at the flashes.

He heard the bunk-house door slam open. Sleepy was running toward him, calling his name. The last flash came from the further corner of the stable front as the shooter darted behind cover. Honey was behind Sleepy, yelling for somebody to tell him what it was all about.

"Stop yellin'!" snapped Hashknife. "One of yuh circle this side of the corral. He's behind the stable. C'mon!"

Sleepy went galloping around the corral, while Hashknife and Honey swung wide of the stable. But the willows and other brush grew down within fifty feet of that side, affording plenty of cover for any one to make a getaway.

After a fifteen-minute search they gave up. It was so dark that a man could merely lie down on the ground and be invisible. They met at the front of the stable, and there they almost stumbled over Slim Coleman, who was sitting up. They heard him swear long and earnestly.

"What in hell happened to you, Slim?" asked Honey.

But Slim merely continued to swear, although he was able to walk back to the bunk-house without assistance. He had a lump over his left ear, a bruised nose, and some skin off his right knuckles.

He blinked in the lamplight and tried to grin.

"Talk about it," urged Honey.

"Talk about it, eh? Well, I dunno what to talk about. After I left the bunk-house I went to git my bronc. Didn't see a danged soul around there, but when I led my horse out I runs slap-dab into somebody. I thought it was one of you boys, comin' out to see if I was gettin' started.

"I started to say somethin', when I got the flash of a six-gun barrel, which almost knocked my nose off. It did jist scrape my nose. I couldn't see the feller very good, but I took a smash at him with my right fist, and I think I hit that gun. And then I got a wallop on the head and I seen all kinds of fireworks. It jist keeled me over, and I 'member tryin' to yell for help. The rest of it is kinda hazy. Whee-e-e! I've shore got me an awful headache."

"But who was it?" wondered Honey. "Is there somebody tryin' to lay yuh out, Slim?"

"Must be. Feel of that bump."

"Honey," said Hashknife, "you better go up to the house and tell the girls what that shootin' was all about. Some of them bullets hit the house. And bring back a pan of hot water, so we can fix Slim's head."

Honey raced for the house and Slim sat down on a bunk. He was still a little dazed.

"Yore bronc is still there by the corral fence," said Sleepy.

"Uh-huh. I still had the lead-rope when I fell. Gee, I shore don't *sabe* it, boys. I dunno anybody that hates me enough to pop me in the dark. It's lucky he didn't hit any of yuh."

"Missed me a mile," grinned Hashknife.

In a few minutes Honey came back carrying a pan of water.

"The girls were scared stiff," he said. "One of them bullets busted the window on this side, and some of the others hit the house. They want me to sleep in the ranch-house."

"I'll bet that makes yuh sore," grinned Sleepy.

"Aw, jist put some horse-liniment on it and I'll head for home," said Slim. "It don't hurt much."

"Yo're not goin' home tonight," declared Hashknife. "This is no night for a tall jigger like you to be ridin'. Shuck off yore raiment and pile into Honey's bunk while me and Sleepy unsaddle yore bronc."

Slim's protests were very feeble.

"Curt Bellew will swear I got drunk and forgot to come home."

"We'll be yore alibi, Slim," assured Hashknife. "And more than that, I'm goin' to need yuh tomorrow."

"Well, all right. Go kinda tender on that pinnacle, cowboy. She's shore a blood-brother to a boil."

Hashknife fixed up Slim's head and then went up to the ranch-house, where he called Honey outside.

"We won't be here for breakfast," he told Honey. "Me and Sleepy and Slim are goin' to take a ride early in the mornin'; *sabe?* They're holdin' that inquest at two o'clock in the afternoon. You hitch up the buggy team in the mornin' and take the girls to town. Tell 'em I said for 'em to go, Honey. Be there for the inquest."

"But what for, Hashknife?"

"Just for fun, Honey. Good-night."

"You'll be at the inquest, won't yuh?"

"Sure, I'm the main witness."

It was an hour before daylight when Hashknife, Sleepy and Slim Coleman rode away from the HJ. Slim's head was a little sore, but the swelling was reduced. Sleepy protested against such an early start; which was the natural thing for him to do, especially since he didn't know where they were going.

They forded the river below the bridge—much to Sleepy's disgust. He got one boot full of water.

"Bridge is too narrow," said Hashknife, "and there's too much brush on the other side of it."

"You must be scared," laughed Sleepy.

The bootful of water made him feel particularly sarcastic. Anyway, he didn't like to ride with an empty stomach.

"Yeah, I'm scared," admitted Hashknife as they reached the other bank and climbed to the top.

"You take the lead, Slim," he said. "Take us to that dead horse."

"All right. It'll be kinda slow goin' in the dark, but it'll be daylight by the time we get there. Got to swing wide of the river on account of the breaks. We can eat breakfast at the Lazy B, if yuh want to."

"We'll look at the horse first, Slim. We may not get any breakfast."

"That's the worst of bein' pardner to a man who is so durned curious he'll get up in the middle of the night to hunt for a dead horse," said Sleepy.

They were obliged to travel slowly, and the cold morning wind caused Sleepy to swear at his wet feet. He was uncomfortable, and didn't care who knew it. The stars faded, and a rosy glow in the east proclaimed the coming of daylight.

Slim knew the country well, and had little difficulty in locating the correct coulee. A coyote streaked out through the brush and went loping off across the hills. He wasn't a bit curious about these cowboys. They often carried rifles, and were not a bit particular which coyote they shot at.

They found the carcass, and Hashknife did not take long in his examination. The other two men sat on their horses some distance away, holding Hashknife's horse. He came back and climbed into his saddle.

"Shall we go to the Lazy B and eat?" asked Slim.

Hashknife shook his head.

"No time to eat, Slim. Is there a place where we can cross the river down here?"

"Yeah, there's the old Circle M crossin'. They herd cattle across once in a while."

"That's fine. Lead us to it."

"You'd think he was a sailor!" wailed Sleepy. "He must be crazy about water. Oh, well, there's no use arguin' with him, Slim."

"You won't miss yore breakfast," assured Hashknife. "If I was as fat as you are I'd welcome a fast."

"I don't mind the breakfast, but I'd like to know what it's all about," said Slim.

"Well, yuh won't know," declared Sleepy. "This jigger never tells. He's a single-handed secret society, he is, Slim."

Hashknife merely laughed and swung in beside them.

"Are yuh pretty good with a six-gun, Slim?"

"Pretty good? Meanin' what, Hartley?"

"Did yuh ever kill a man?"

"Nope." Slim shook his head violently. "Never had to."

"Would, if yuh had to, wouldn't yuh?"

"Sure—why not?"

"Yuh may have to."

Sleepy straightened up in his saddle. Slim looked quickly at Sleepy who was grinning widely. Sleepy always grinned when there was action in the wind.

"I don't quite *sabe* the drift of this, Hartley," said Slim. "Why should I have to kill a man?"

"To make him quit shootin'."

"Oh, yeah. Well—all right."

Slim drew his six-shooter, examined the cylinder critically and put it back.

"I wish I'd a' practised more," he said dryly.

Hashknife grinned in appreciation. He felt that Slim was a dependable man. They reached the west bank of the river and rode south for about a quarter of a mile to the Circle M crossing. The water was not deep here.

Old cottonwoods grew close to the water edge and there were many cattle standing among the trees. The cowboys rode out to the open country, almost within sight of the Circle M. Hashknife studied the country. Farther on and to their left was a rather high butte, fairly well covered with brush.

"On the other side of that is the Circle M road, ain't it?" asked Hashknife.

Slim nodded.

"Circles the bottom of it on that side. It's only a little ways to the Circle M. There's a little stream comes down on this side of the butte, and the road crosses it."

Hashknife took the lead now. He rode to the south of the butte, dismounted at the foot and tied his horse in the thick brush. The other boys followed him, and they walked up through the brush to the top of the butte.

Below, and not over four hundred yards to the south, were the ranch buildings of the Circle M. Hashknife squatted down on a rocky projection and told the others to keep out of sight. There was enough high brush to make an effectual screen.

The ranch-house of the Circle M was a rambling affair consisting of but one floor. The exterior was rough boards, weathered, unpainted. There were two stables and a number of low sheds, branding corral, bucking corral and general utility corrals. A number of loose horses were in the larger corral.

Smoke was pouring from the kitchen stovepipe, and in a few minutes a man came from the stable and went to the house.

"That's Ben Collins," said Slim. "I know his walk."

"Have they got a Chink cook?" asked Sleepy.

"Nope. Dutch Siebert does most of the cookin'. He's a puncher. Ed never could keep a cook, it seems, so he uses Dutch. He's an awful flat-head."

"Merrick?"

"No—Siebert. Danged flat-faced, obstinate sort of a cuss."

Sleepy stretched out on the ground and pillowed his head on his arms.

"Wake me up early, mother; I'm to be queen of the May," he grinned. "If yuh won't tell me what we're doin' here, I'm goin' to take a nap. Yuh might as well sleep, Slim."

"Go ahead," said Hashknife. "I'll wake yuh up in time."

Slim needed no second invitation, but slid out full length.

Hashknife made himself comfortable, but not to sleep. He kept an eye on the ranch-buildings, and several times he saw Merrick and Collins together. He knew Merrick well enough to distinguish him at that distance.

Time dragged on and the sun grew hot up there on the top of that knoll, but Hashknife had the patience of an Indian. It was nearly eleven o'clock when he saw Merrick and Collins saddle their horses at the corral. A third man came out from the house and talked with them, and Hashknife was sure this man was Dutch Siebert. He was bigger than either of the other two, who were fairly big men.

In a little while Merrick and Collins mounted their horses and moved away from the ranch on the road which led to Pinnacle City. They were going to attend the inquest. Hashknife paid no more attention to them, but noted the time of their leaving and estimated about how long it would take them to reach the town. Dutch Siebert played with a dog in the yard for a few minutes, then went into the house.

Hashknife settled back and rolled a cigarette. Sleepy woke up, swore a few lines, shifted to more shade and went back to sleep. But Hashknife did not become impatient. He knew what he was going to do, and it was something that required fairly accurate timing. He knew that Merrick and Collins would ride fairly fast and would cover that eight miles in less than an hour.

It was thirty minutes past the noon hour when Hashknife woke Sleepy and Slim. Both required some stretching to get the kinks out of their muscles. Hashknife led the way back to the horses, where they mounted, and circled around to the road near the place where the little stream crossed it. Hashknife dismounted at the stream. They were almost in view of the ranch, the main gate being just around a brushy turn in the road.

Sleepy was curious as to what Hashknife intended doing, and his curiosity was even greater when he saw Hashknife take a chunk of yellow soap from his pocket.

"What'sa big idea, cowboy?" he asked. "Goin' to take a bath?"

"Git off and help me," grinned Hashknife.

They dismounted and Sleepy held the horse while Hashknife filled his hat with water, poured it over the shoulders of the animal and began rubbing in the soap.

"The idea is," grunted Hashknife, "to make us look like we've come to beat—!"

"Lather, eh?" grunted Slim. "Gimme half that soap, and I'll fix up this side. You hold the rollin' stock, Sleepy."

It did not take long for them to make that horse look as if it had run many miles. They splashed and rubbed until Hashknife stepped back and grinned his appreciation. Then he scooped up a double handful of dust, threw it in the air and let it settle on him, like white ash.

"All right, boys," he said swinging into the saddle. "Stay where yuh are until I go past. Then leave yore broncs here and sneak in, keepin' under cover. If I need yuh, you'll get a signal. Now, get back, 'cause I'm goin' to throw dust."

He rode back about two hundred yards, swung the horse around and came past them as fast as the horse could run. The pounding hoofs threw dust all over them, but they tied their horses and ran along the road, keeping against the brush.

Hashknife did not slacken speed, until almost at the door of the ranch-house. Big Dutch Siebert stepped to the doorway and the sliding hoofs slithered gravel against the half-open door.

Hashknife's coming was so sudden that the Dutchman did not seem to know just what to do. And Hashknife was out of the saddle and around to Dutch almost before the horse came to a stop. Hashknife took one keen look back up the road, whirled on Dutch and stepped to the threshold.

"Get inside—quick!" snapped Hashknife.

Siebert stepped back quickly. He was a huge man, flat of face, narrow-eyed, one side of his mouth sagging from a big chew of tobacco. Once his big right hand swayed back past his holstered gun, but came away. He was being rushed so fast he didn't have time to think. And Dutch Siebert was not a fast thinker.

"Ed sent me!" snapped Hashknife. "He didn't dare to come, because they're watchin' him. There's been a leak, Dutch. Ed says to get Joe out of here as fast as yuh can, because they're comin' to search the place. You know what that means? Hurry up, you fool; they're comin'!"

Siebert gasped foolishly, whirled on his heel and almost ran into the kitchen. He grasped the heavy kitchen table, whirled it aside and started to drop to one knee. Then he swung around. Dutch Siebert was beginning to think. His hand jerked back to his gun, but he moved too late.

Hashknife was on top of him, driving him against the wall, while Hashknife's right hand, gripping a heavy gun, described a short downward arc, and Dutch Siebert ceased to think for a while.

Hashknife picked up Dutch's gun, ran to the doorway and wig-wagged wildly with both arms. Sleepy and Slim broke from the fringe of brush and came running across the yard.

"One of yuh go to the stable and get a rope!" yelled Hashknife.

Sleepy veered off and headed for the stable.

"Did the soap and water work?" asked Slim, panting from his run.

"It always works," grinned Hashknife. "C'mon in."

CHAPTER IX:
THE INQUEST

"Have you seen anythin' of Slim Coleman, Len?" Curt Bellew leaned in through the doorway of the sheriff's office and spoke to Kelsey, who was oiling a gun.

"Ain't seen him," said Kelsey shortly.

"That's funny. He started for town yesterday. I've been all over this darned place and I can't find him and nobody has seen him."

Kelsey did not show much interest, so Curt snorted and walked away. He was a little worried about Slim. Honey Bee and the two girls drove into town and left their rig at the livery-stable. Uncle Hozie and Aunt Emma were in town, and the old lady immediately took charge of the girls, much to Honey's relief, because he didn't know what to do with them.

The Heavenly Triplets were in town but were keeping strictly sober. One reason was that they were not only broke but badly in debt. The morning train had brought the conductor, brakeman and fireman of the cattle-train to identify the dead brakeman, and to testify at the inquest.

Curt Bellew, still looking for the missing Slim, ran into Honey Bee. It seemed that everybody in town knew by this time that Slim was missing.

"Aw, he was at the HJ all night," said Honey. "He was goin' home, all right, Curt, but somebody bent a gun over his head. By golly, we had quite a shootin' scrape out there! Somebody emptied a gun at Hashknife Hartley, but didn't touch him."

"Honey, you ain't lyin', are yuh?" asked Curt. There were several interested listeners.

"I shore ain't, Curt," declared Honey. "Slim needed a little patchin' up, but he's all right."

"Where is he now?"

"I can't tell yuh, Curt—because I don't know m'self."

Several questions were fired at Honey, but he had the same answer for each. In the meantime Curt went back to Kelsey's office and asked him whether he had heard about the shooting at the HJ.

"What shootin', Curt?"

Curt told him what Honey had said about it.

"Why would anybody hit Slim Coleman?" asked Kelsey.

"That's the question without any answer."

"Where are Hartley and Stevens?"

"I dunno. Mebbe they're with Slim."

Ed Merrick and Ben Collins rode in from the Circle M, and heard about Slim's experience before they had their horses tied. Abe Liston of the 3W3 gave them the news.

"By Gee, they can't lay that on to Joe Rich," declared Abe. "Slim and Joe were darned good friends."

"Where's Slim now?" asked Merrick.

"Nobody knows, except that he's with them other punchers at the HJ. Honey Bee and the two girls just came in a while ago, and Honey says he don't know where they are."

Merrick found Honey a little later and asked him about the incident. He told Merrick about the same story Abe had told, except that he elaborated on the shooting in the dark between Hashknife and the unknown gunman.

"Well, what do yuh make of it?" asked Merrick.

"I don't know," laughed Honey. "Looks like somebody had gone plumb crazy."

"Does look like it, Honey. What did Hartley think?"

"That feller never says what he thinks, Ed. He bandaged Slim's head and made him stay all night. Slim wanted to go home, but Hashknife told him it was a bad night for a tall cowpuncher to be ridin' around.

"Him and Sleepy and Slim pulled out before daylight, but didn't tell me where they were goin'. Yuh never can find out anythin' from Hashknife. He just grins at yore questions. It's a wonder they didn't accuse me of bustin' Slim."

Honey laughed and grimaced at the thought.

"Accuse you?" queried Merrick.

"Yeah. Yuh see, Slim ruined my supper. He told me about findin' a horse that had been skinned. Why, anybody would skin a horse is a mystery to me. But anyway, they got to talkin' about that dead horse. Hashknife was interested, it seemed, and when Slim saw it was botherin' me, they went strong."

Merrick laughed shortly.

"Yeah, it's a wonder they didn't accuse yuh of hittin' him. Mebbe they went to look at the dead horse."

"I wouldn't put it past 'em," laughed Honey. "But they'll be here for the inquest, Ed."

Even with the range well represented in Pinnacle City there was not a great deal of interest in the inquest over the body of the brakeman. He was a stranger, and there was but one verdict to be brought in. It would merely be a matter of form. In fact, the rewards were already printed, charging Joe Rich with the murder and offering thirty-five hundred dollars for him dead or alive, or for information that would lead to his arrest. It did not mention conviction. As far as that goes, he was already convicted.

Old Doctor Curzon decided to hold the inquest in a court-room. The crowd was too large for his little home and the county would not pay him for trampled flowerbeds. The body had already been identified by the trainmen. Aunt Emma, Peggy and Laura had taken seats in the Flying H wagon. They were not going up to the court-room. Aunt Emma wanted to find Honey and make him take the girls back home.

"Why did he bring you?" demanded the old lady. "With all this talk goin' on! I'll sure tell him where to head in!"

"I think it was Hashknife's idea, Auntie," said Peggy wearily.

"It was, eh? And who's he to tell you what to do? The sooner you quit cryin' over Joe Rich the better you'll be off. After all he's done to you! Peggy, you ought to have sense."

"There comes Hashknife now!" exclaimed Peggy.

It seemed like a cry of hope. Something seemed to tell her that this tall cowboy riding up the middle of the street, sitting very straight in his saddle, was bringing a ray of sunshine.

He did not seem interested in the crowd. Straight to the hitch-rack he came, dismounted slowly and tied the horse.

As he stepped away from the animal he saw the three women in the wagon and smiled at them as he touched the brim of his hat with his right hand. They watched him angle across the street, going toward the sheriff's office. Kelsey and Angus McLaren were coming from the office and stopped to speak with Hashknife. After a few moments of conversation they saw Kelsey turn and go back to the office with Hashknife.

Peggy kept her eyes glued to the office door, disregarding the advice of Aunt Emma, who was telling her what she should do. In a few minutes Hashknife came slowly outside and back up the street. It was two o'clock.

Near the entrance of the court-house Hashknife met the Heavenly Triplets, who were anxious to get a front seat. He said something to Lonnie Myers, and after a few moments the three men followed him farther up the street, where they held a short, earnest conversation. Following the conversation the three men went back to the court-house and went inside.

Hashknife leaned against the front of the general store and rolled a smoke. Jack Ralston and Buck West crossed the street from the Pinnacle Saloon, and Hashknife called to Jack. The deputy came over to him and they held a short conversation, after which they headed for the sheriff's office and went inside.

"There's something going on," declared Peggy. "But where are Sleepy and Slim, do you suppose?"

"I can't even suppose," replied Aunt Emma. "I hope that inquest won't take long. Hozie will stay until the last dog is hung, you may be sure of that. And us out here in this hot sun. But that's a man for yuh!"

"You came in for the inquest, didn't you, Aunt Emma?" asked Laura.

"I did not—Hozie did. I have no interest in things of that kind."

"There is Hashknife now!" exclaimed Peggy.

The tall cowboy was standing at the door of the court-house, and none of them had seen him leave the sheriff's office. After a few moments of deliberation, he went in and climbed the stairs.

The rather spacious court-room was not filled. There were possibly fifty people in the room. Lonnie Myers stood near the doorway at the top of the stairs; Dan Leach was at the opposite corner, at the rear; while Nebrasky Jones sat in a front seat, very erect and very dignified.

Doctor Curzon had already selected a jury when Hashknife came in; and the six men, Cut Bellew, Eph Harper, Jimmy Black of the 3W3, Buck West, Fred Thornton, a feed-store keeper, and Jud Albertson, a blacksmith, were occupying the jury-box.

Fred Coburn, the prosecuting attorney, was the only lawyer in the room. Hashknife moved down to the front and took the only available seat. Across the aisle from him sat Ben Collins. Farther back and across the aisle sat Merrick and Angus McLaren, the Circle M owner on the outside seat.

Old Doctor Curzon conferred with the attorney for several moments before calling the inquest to order.

"I believe we will have the testimony of the sheriff first," he said, looking around the room.

But neither the sheriff nor deputy were in evidence.

"Will some one call the sheriff?" asked Coburn.

Hashknife got slowly to his feet and half turned in the narrow aisle, where his glance swept the audience. His face seemed a little pale and his lips were shut tightly. Then—

"The sheriff won't be here," he said distinctly. "Neither will the deputy. Their evidence is locked up, and I've got the key in my pocket."

For several moments the room was hushed.

"I don't believe we quite understand you," said Coburn.

"It was plain English," replied Hashknife.

"But—but—" spluttered the attorney. No one else spoke; all were too interested for words.

"So we'll jist have to do without 'em," said Hashknife. "Yuh see, I'm playin' safe, folks."

His lips twisted to a grin, but his eyes were cold, mirthless.

"This is an inquest over the body of a murdered man, a man who was shot down in the performance of his duty, and he was killed at a time when the lives of a lot of folks might have been at stake.

"You've merely met here as a matter of form to make it legal to hunt down and destroy Joe Rich. Ain't I right?"

"Perfectly!" snapped the attorney.

"Uh-huh. Well, how would it be to git a little of that testimony from a real interested party?" Hashknife glanced toward the doorway.

"C'mon in," he said loudly.

The crowd surged around in their seats, gasping in amazement. Joe Rich was limping down the aisle. He was clad in an old gray shirt and pair of bib-overalls, old misfitting shoes; his unshaven face, dirty; hair matted. A gasp went up from the crowd as Joe halted beside Hashknife and turned to look at them. He appeared years older, weak. His eyes were bloodshot, and the wrists below the shirt-sleeves were scored from rope burns.

"The main witness," said Hashknife. "Look him over, folks. Does he look like a man who had killed and robbed?"

Still the crowd did not move. They seemed content to sit still and gaze at the man. Then a man strangled, a chair rattled. It was Ed Merrick the owner of the Circle M. He had whirled in his chair and started for the door, running like a drunken man, but his way was blocked by Sleepy, Slim Coleman and Lonnie Myers and three guns were shoved in his face.

He stopped, staggered sidewise and whirled around, his gun in his hand. But before he could use it, Sleepy and Lonnie landed on him with a rush and he went down, struggling wildly.

Ben Collins had not moved. He merely flinched when Hashknife leaned across him and took away his gun. He seemed in a daze.

"Got him!" panted Sleepy.

Hashknife looked toward the doorway. Peggy was coming in, her eyes wide, staring down at Joe who had not seen her. Slim touched her on the arm, but she did not stop.

Hashknife beckoned her and she ran down the aisle. Joe turned and saw her coming toward him and the next moment he had her in his arms, while Hashknife hastily sidestepped and took Ben Collins by the arm.

"C'mon, Collins," he said. "You need exercise."

"Lemme have him," said Nebrasky. "Me and Dan can handle him real good. I've got a rope handy."

"All right, Nebrasky."

Hashknife turned to face the prosecuting attorney.

"What is this all about?" he demanded. "Don't you realise what—"

"Better than anybody else," smiled Hashknife. "Here," he handed a key to Dan Leach. "There's two more cells empty. Put Collins in one and Merrick in the other."

"Well, I'll be darned!" That was about as near as Fred Coburn ever came to using profanity.

Uncle Hozie was pawing at Hashknife, masticating violently and staring at Joe Rich and Peggy.

"Wh-what about him?" demanded Uncle Hozie, pointing at Joe.

"Oh, don't bother 'em," grinned Hashknife. "Listen, you folks. I've got the whole story. Dutch Siebert is hog-tied at the Circle M and we found Joe Rich in a cellar under the house, where he's been since the day he rode out of town.

"Joe Rich didn't get drunk on his weddin' night. He took two drinks of liquor with Len Kelsey in the Arapho saloon, and Len slipped him some knockout drops. Joe knew he hadn't been drunk, but there wasn't any way to prove it. Merrick practically forced Joe to appoint Kelsey and it was Merrick's idea to discredit Joe in order to make Kelsey sheriff. Merrick wanted to own the law.

"Well, he done a rattlin' good job of it. In fact, he overdone his job. That bridge wasn't hit by lightning; it was set on fire to let Merrick get off that express car after he had robbed the safe. Collins and Dutch Siebert were there with the horses, and they set the fire. The brakeman ran into 'em and they killed him. Anybody with any sense would have known it couldn't be a one-man job. The man who robbed that safe couldn't have killed the brakeman, because he was put out of the way before the train stopped.

"And Joe Rich did not rob Jim Wheeler. That was done by Siebert and Collins, after Merrick had given Wheeler just one thousand dollars. Merrick made out two notes, and Jim Wheeler thought one was a duplicate. He read his own—and signed Merrick's, which read 'five thousand.' But Jim Wheeler lost his note, and I found it under the sidewalk, over there by the Pinnacle Saloon. I don't know how they found it out, but I reckon they did, because last night they mistook Slim Coleman for me and batted him over the head.

"But they overdone the evidence part at both the train and at the bank. I didn't know Joe Rich, but from what I could learn he was intelligent—too danged intelligent to wear those leather cuffs, lose a knife with his initials on it and all that. Merrick and Jack Ralston caught Joe that first day. That is, they downed his horse, and took him to the Circle M. They had to skin that animal to keep anybody from seein' it was Joe's horse.

"And here's the particularly devilish part of it all. They were tryin' to pile up a big reward, soak Joe with a murder charge and make it dead or alive. Know what that means? It means that they were going to kill Joe and get that money, make heroes out of themselves and live happy for a long time on the money they've got in that cellar. That's the story, folks."

The room was in an uproar following the finish of the story. They wanted to get outside where there was more room to talk. But Hashknife knew they were going to do more than talk. They were clattering down the stairs when Hashknife touched Joe on the arm.

"Get down there," he said softly. "Yo're the sheriff yet, Joe—Kelsey's disqualified. Stop 'em at the door. They'll listen to yuh, kid."

Joe ran from the room and they heard him going down the steps. Peggy was looking at Hashknife, her eyes filled with tears, as she held out her hands to him.

"Oh, it was wonderful," she said. "But I knew you would do something wonderful; I knew it, Hashknife."

"Yeah," he said bashfully. "It worked out pretty good."

"Oh, I don't know how you did it, Hashknife. Everybody was against Joe. Why did you think he was innocent? What made you think it was a plot against him?"

"I looked at you," said Hashknife simply. "And I figured that a man you'd love—well, I figured right, Peggy."

They went down the stairs. A crowd had gathered in front of the sheriff's office, and Joe was talking to them, backed against the door. He was flanked on one side by Slim Coleman, and on the other by Honey Bee. And then the crowd began to disperse. Aunt Emma and Peggy met them at the bottom of the stairs and Laura kissed Hashknife before he was aware of her intentions.

Angus McLaren came up to Hashknife and held out his hand.

"Har-rtley, I've nothin' to say. Ye take my breath away. If I've anythin' to say about it—Joe's still sheriff. He talked 'em out of usin' ropes, and he's suffered enough to entitle him to somethin'. And there's a reward for ye, man—the money that was offered for Joe Rich. We've got him back, and he's worth every cent we're payin' for him."

Hashknife smiled and shook his head.

"We don't want money, McLaren—only enough for two fares East. The rest will help Peggy start housekeepin' with the man she kept on lovin', in spite of hell and high water."

"Two fares East?" queried McLaren.

"Yeah. Yuh see, we missed our train the night we came."

"Oh, I see."

"And Sleepy will like it, yuh know. I have to kinda humour him once in a while."

"But you're not going away for years and years," declared Peggy. "Not after what you've done, Hashknife. Stay here in the Tumbling River with all of us."

"Ye fit well in here," said McLaren.

"And here comes Joe," said Laura. "We'll see what he has to say about you going away, Mister Man."

"And you tell me some time," smiled Hashknife. "It'll keep."

He hurried away to find Sleepy, who was regaling a crowd with a story of the lathered horse.

"It's shore funny how things work out," he said. "Here we were headin' East for a little trip, and all this happens."

"Are yuh goin' to keep on headin' East?" asked one of the crowd.

"Not us," said Sleepy. "I'm all out of the notion."

Hashknife turned and went across the street, where he intercepted McLaren.

"We've changed our minds about goin' East," he said. "We'll take a couple of horses and saddles instead of them tickets, McLaren."

"All right," laughed McLaren. "Where are you goin', lad?"

"Somewhere on the other side of the hill."

"What hill, Hartley?"

"The next one," smiled Hashknife.